I0762087

FLEETING NOTE

By Sherban Young

THE ENESCU FLEET SERIES

Fleeting Memory
Fleeting Glance
Fleeting Note
Fleeting Chance
Fleeting Promise

THE WARREN KINGSLEY SERIES

Five Star Detour
Double Cover

MORE BOOKS

Opportunity Slips
Dead Men Do Tell Tales

FLEETING NOTE

AN ENESCU FLEET MYSTERY

SHERBAN YOUNG

Columbia, MD

Cover and illustrations by Katerina Vamvasaki

Editing services by Katherine Richards from *The Reading Panda*

ISBN-10: 0-9912324-5-3
EAN-13: 978-0-9912324-5-1

MysteryCaper Press
Columbia, Maryland

www.mysterycaper.com
www.sherbanyoung.com

Dedication

To Rachel Barton Pine

For graciously making time to consult on this project
and for a delightful evening of Paganini

Acknowledgments

I would like to thank my Romanian connections, Sheilah Kast and Ernest Latham, as well as Eric Neffke at the Enoch Pratt Free Library for his excellent research.

1 — Treacherous Prelude

I raised my drink once again. It was mostly ice by now—a trace of tonic, very little gin—but it didn't matter. I took a long and thoughtful slurp, giving the contents an idle rattle as I brought the excess back down to the snarled tablecloth at my elbow.

I found the act soothing.

When my friend Enescu Fleet, the internationally renowned (semi-retired) private detective, told me last week that the prestigious Pendleton Institute in Baltimore wanted to honor him at a banquet and we were all invited as his guests, I was perplexed. I couldn't figure why an elite music college would want to toast a private eye, no matter how famous and semiretired he may be. When he later explained, the night of the banquet, that the celebration was not so much in recognition of his feats as an aging gentleman gumshoe but, in fact, in tribute to his esteemed Romanian ancestor, the composer George Enescu, I was up to speed. Up to speed and careening headlong toward the figurative orchestra pit.

Fleet, you see, wasn't related to the composer Enescu. He wasn't even Romanian.

Why his parents chose to christen him Enescu of all things no one really knew. But the fact remained that his folks had lived and loved without a drop of Romanian blood in them, let alone Enescu blood, and as far as I was aware Fleet hadn't picked up any in the last six decades.

That was the predicament he had landed in our neatly pressed laps.

True to form, he hadn't spoken a word of this until our party was well inside, basking in the architectural scope of the Pendleton Library.

"A moment, Johnny, before we locate our table," he had remarked then, and in a few quick words had filled me in.

I hadn't flinched. I was used to his methods. I took my seat, smiled at my fellow Enescu aficionados, and quietly ordered a pitcher of gin.

I could see the evening stretching out ahead of us: embarrassment, ridicule, a snub by our social betters, and potentially getting sent home without any after-dinner sorbet. It wasn't a charming prospect.

And yet, as I sat there an hour later, calmly watching my ice melt, I realized none of this had actually happened. He had carried it off. I don't know why I was surprised. He always managed somehow, that guy.

His triumph hadn't come without trade-offs, of course. A touch of drama. A vase of decorative orchids that would never be the same. One fairly unpleasant corpse…

But now I'm getting ahead of myself.

We arrived at the banquet at around six that evening. We were all dolled up and ready for a night of refined merriment. Fleet's personal guest list consisted of his daughter, Ate, only too pleased to show her father her support; our friend Hutton, glad to go anywhere Ate went; my fiancée, Lesley, happy for the opportunity to scope out venues for our wedding; and me. I had no ulterior motives for attending. And now that I knew the true nature of tonight's honor, or rather its false nature, I definitely wasn't happy, glad or pleased.

I held nothing back from the table. Seconds after Fleet had shared his tidbit, I leaned in and whispered the details to Lesley, who whispered them to Ate, who whispered to Hutton, who whispered to a waiter to bring more gin.

The question of the hour became *Why?* Why accept a distinguished public honor, assemble an entourage, and basically prepare to whoop it up in that vein, when you knew perfectly well it—the distinguished public honor—had nothing to do with you.

This fell to me to ask. I would have preferred more of a team effort, an "intervention" if you like, but the ladies were too busy discussing the feasibility of making a break for it in their heels, while Hutton and the waiter were still threshing out the true nature of an open bar.

"Why?" echoed Enescu Fleet.

"Why," I agreed, drumming my fork on the tablecloth.

He mused on this a moment. "You're too young to appreciate this, Johnny, but when you get to be my age you'll understand what it means to yearn for excitement in your golden years. A life such as mine—sedate, unadventurous—calls for a little stimulation from time to time. You need to pounce on any passing thrill you can. I'm not ashamed to admit that when this offer came along, I pounced on it like a starving puma."

I said ha!, pouncing on this explanation like a puma who didn't believe a word he was hearing. Sedate and unadventurous, my neatly pressed rear end! The only thing more ridiculous than Enescu Fleet calling his life sedate and unadventurous would be James Bond claiming he needed to get out of the office a bit more often—meet some girls, possibly brush up on his baccarat. I had a feeling there was something Fleet wasn't telling me here.

Before I could dig any deeper, a gang of roving classical music fans materialized at the table and he stood to engage them in conversation.

He certainly fit right in among posh society. Something about his wry expression, the wave in his hair, the salt-and-pepper of his beard—they just seemed to go with the formal duds. He looked like a cover for *GQ* (the Geezer Rapscallion edition).

The rest of us weren't exactly straight out of the clothing hamper, mind you. Hutton and I made a perfectly acceptable presentation in our dinner jackets. It went without saying that Ate and Lesley took the breath away in their slinky, cleavage-revealing evening wear (the cleavage was the best part). But it was Fleet who scooped in the trophy for simple urbanity. He appeared more comfortable in his gleaming tuxedo than most men do in sweatpants and a T-shirt.

He resumed his seat, having sent the groupies on their way, and we continued our chat. That is, I scowled and shook my head while he smoothed the lines of his well-groomed beard. I saw him half smile and assumed his conscience must have said something droll.

"You're frowning, Johnny. Have you run out of gin?"

I had, but that wasn't why I frowned. Realizing I hadn't made much of a success out of the *Why*, I changed chords and went with *How*. "How are you going to pull this off?" I asked.

"You have doubts?"

"Gobs."

"Well, dismiss them from your mind. These revelries never prove very challenging. A word or two from our distinguished guest speaker and it's all over in ten minutes." It sounded like he had impersonated distant relatives of prominent Romanian composers before.

I gaped. "You have to make a speech?" For some reason, this hadn't occurred to me.

"Naturally. I suppose I should get working on that," he said.

I sloshed what was left of my cocktail. "You haven't prepared anything!"

He dismissed the question from our minds. He never prepared speeches ahead of time. Ruined the spontaneity. "Besides, if I get in a jam, I can always tell them the one about Stokowski."

I blinked at him.

"The conductor, Leopold Stokowski," he clarified. He went on to explain that he had an anecdote about this Stokowski, and it would have the audience rolling in the aisles—which were black-and-white marble, I noticed, with a slight art deco design to the tile.

Although it delighted me to hear that he would be keeping things in a musical motif, I was curious how an anecdote about the conductor Stokowski, or any brand of Stokowski, was going to sway the constituents from his appointed speech about the composer Enescu. I would have asked him to shed some light on this, but by then he had already left for the podium.

We had begun.

2 — Rhapsody in Red

There was a short stage wait first as Fleet shook hands with various music-school muckety-mucks. This included a round old duffer who looked like a dean; a less-round duffer who looked like an assistant dean; a silver-haired lady in sequins who, to her credit, didn't look like a dean or assistant dean; and finally a younger woman in cobalt silk, who could have been the minder for any of the other three, but was, in reality, the up-and-coming Victoria Walters.

I learned this from the school magazine under my chair. Victoria Walters had assumed the role of orchestral director at the college this spring, and great things were expected from her. I wondered if she had heard the one about Stokowski.

The introductions out of the way, the powers that be had now formed a makeshift huddle alongside the platform. They were most likely reviewing the evening's agenda: deciding who should speak first, who should make the introductions, and what to do if the opposition rushed the line of scrimmage. Figuring this might go on for a few minutes, I let my eyes roam around the cavernous Pendleton Library.

On any other occasion, I would have sat back in awe of the joint. Built in 1865 (magazine under chair), it represented the crown jewel of the Pendleton campus. Roughly a billion square feet (personal estimate), it was made up of rows of exquisitely carved stone columns; buttresses, both flying and not as flying; ivory and golden accents; and a giant tiled skylight. It was available for weddings, bar mitzvahs and distinguished guest speakers of questionable descent.

I set the magazine down and looked upwards. Without a doubt, the library's most striking feature, the skin and bones of the colossus, was its network of balconies. Encircling the room were three…four… five…let's go with five stories of balconies. They were coffee colored in their patina, very ornate and home to one…two…something like three hundred thousand ancient texts.

I was still gazing up at these, speculating how long it would take a person to read them all, when I had the sensation that someone was watching me. This had been going on for the last couple minutes, I would say: that sense that I was guilty of some egregious social gaffe and, as a result, a pair of eyes were boring hard into the back of my head. Lesley was still conferring with Ate on the mental state of the latter's father, so it had to be somebody else.

It was.

Turning, I observed a man about my age, dressed all in black and glaring toward our table. By the way he was hunkered over his place setting you could see he was a bruiser even before he stood. He did this now, replacing his napkin on his plate and heading in our direction. He had to be six foot nine, all sable limbs and flowing black hair.

I couldn't help noticing that Hutton's eyebrow twitched as the man approached.

You wouldn't know it from the typical look on my friend's face—detached, mildly amused by most everything he encountered—but Hutton was deceptively aware of his surroundings. As a PI himself, following in the footsteps of Enescu Fleet (in more ways than one), this wasn't a bad trait to have.

He shot another glance out from behind his Buddy Holly-style specs and drew himself up in his seat.

His expression indicated that he had been watching our watcher for some time: probably a goodly while if even I had spotted him. (Typically I'm pretty much as aware of my surroundings as you would expect from the look on my face.)

The guy dropped anchor between us. "Well, if it isn't E. F. Hutton," he announced. "When did the Pendleton Institute start lowering its standards?"

My time spent in the company of two private detectives—twice the daily dose of detectives for the average consumer—has honed my skills as an observer and deducer. I might not notice everything around me, nor do I usually have any clue what is going on in an investigation, but I do pick up on more than most.

Because of this, I could infer several things about our new arrival. Judging from his accent, he was British, possibly Welsh. The fact that he referred to my friend as *E. F. Hutton* suggested he had been at school with us, which was where the Hutton moniker had been born. Lastly, from the sneering way in which he spoke, and a little bit his hairdo, I could deduce that he was something of a dick-weed. Of my three conclusions, I felt my investigative technique was most on the money with that one.

My second theory, that he must have gone to school with us, was also soon confirmed. I didn't remember him myself, thank God, but Hutton apparently knew him quite well (and seemed to wish he didn't).

It never ceases to amaze me how a person's disposition can alter completely around certain peers, especially peers from the past. I'd known Hutton over twenty years, and from boyhood on his demeanor could best be described as aristocratic. Polished. In command. Today the aristocrat had gone straight out of him. He barely spoke, letting this schoolyard relic dominate the conversation. When he did participate, his replies were short and plain and noticeably heavy on British phraseology. I didn't like it.

I didn't like our newcomer much either. Chester "Chet" Callas—for that was his name—wasn't everybody's cup of gin. Since last seen, he had become a classical music critic for some stuffy British music magazine, and he wanted us to know that he was an outstanding critic. Revered by all. An unparalleled analyst of sound.

He was a dick-weed.

It turned out that he didn't remember me any more than I remembered him. I was okay with this. I had no desire to be remembered by a man who dressed in a black silk tuxedo shirt, wore a closely trimmed vandyke beard, and spent more time brushing and teasing his hair than I did growing mine.

He didn't just resemble a Restoration Era pimp, he acted the part too. Already he had given our womenfolk a long and studied leer, like a man perusing a mail-order bride catalog; and when Fleet's daughter introduced herself, he leaned into Hutton and asked him if he was getting any of that.

Hutton, I'm pleased to report, declined to reply to this. Good for him, I say. Too much of that going on these days. There used to be a time when you didn't bandy a woman's name. Besides, I happened to know he wasn't getting any, so what would have been the point?

"So you're the old bloke's daughter, then?" Chet inquired.

Ate raised her head from her champagne flute. She was Enescu Fleet's daughter, yes.

"Long-lost relatives of George Enescu?"

"That's right." She spoke emphatically, the pride of a million Romanian daughters coming before her. I was glad someone at the table had some vigor. True, she wasn't a Romanian daughter, and her words only perpetuated her father's fabrication, but anything was better than giving this snake a leg up—not that snakes generally have legs.

The serpent grinned. "I believe someone is having a laugh."

"And what's that supposed to mean?"

Chet said it wasn't important—only that her dear old dad was no more related to George Enescu than he was to the Prince of Wales. (See, I knew he was Welsh.)

"It's like those cases of his," he chuckled. "I've read about them. Victims leaving behind cryptic clues to their own murders. Elaborate riddles fingering killers from beyond the grave. Rubbish. Nobody would get on like that in real life. In real life, dead men tell no tales. They simply kick off, and that's that. You and I both know these things get embellished in the press."

Ate assured him that no such embellishment had taken place in this instance. If anything, her father's investigations had been more remarkable than the press had documented.

I concurred. As one who had done some of that documenting, I could tell them that Enescu Fleet's investigations had been pretty remarkable. Out of context, they probably came off as rather far-fetched—on two separate occasions a murder victim leaving behind a puzzle that would later lead us to the solution of the mystery—but that was how they happened. They were a hoot.

Chet ignored my testimony and gave hers another smirky smile. "What was your name again, luv? Abby?"

"Ate."

"Addie?"

"Ate. A-T-E. It's pronounced *Ah-tee.*"

Chet wagged his raven locks at her. "That doesn't work for me at all. If we were friends, I'd have to insist on pronouncing it *Āt*, as in *ate,* the past tense of *eat.*"

"Fortunately, we're not friends," said Ate, the present tense of pissed off.

"I mean, I don't see where you're getting this *Ah-tee* stuff," snorted Chet.

"I'm named for the goddess Atë."

"Are you, just?"

"I am, just," she retorted, the strain growing in her voice. It wouldn't have taken much more, I knew, for her to slip off one of her stiletto heels and spear the guy in the forehead.

"Tell him about the bing-bongs," I suggested, hoping to ease the situation.

The table stared at me.

"The little bing-bongs," I explained. "Over the *e.*"

When I first met Ate, a little less than a year ago, she had placed a great deal of emphasis on these bing-bongs. The goddess Atë, it seemed, had these two whosits over the *ë—bing-bongs—*and even though the modern Ate spurned these decorative touches, this little splash of backstory had always helped me remember that there was more to her name than met the eye.

Chet remained unimpressed. "You'd know best of course," he sniffed at her. "But I'll always think of you as *ate.* In fact, if you ever decide to murder me, I'll pay tribute to this by holding out four fingers on each hand. Get it? Four and four makes *eight.*"

Ate said she got it. *Eight.* Sounds like *ate.* Just like one of her father's cases. Perhaps someday they would have a chance to put this promise into practice, she remarked.

Chet removed an antique pocket watch from his waistcoat (and here I was thinking he was some kind of dandy). He glanced at the time, then at the podium, and then back at the watch. He looked very bored by it all. "I would have thought we'd have started by now."

Hutton, breaking his vow of silence, said he would have thought so too. Perhaps they were having mic trouble. Nine times out of ten, he pointed out, a delay on stage is due to a bollocks with the mic.

Lesley said maybe so. But that shouldn't prevent our visitor from returning to his table. Ate agreed. Go promptly was her advice.

Chet ignored these digs. "You have to understand," he sighed, "I'm all keyed up to hear about the wondrous Great-Uncle George."

The name got my attention. I flinched in my seat, twirling this way then that. "Uncle George? Where?"

I should explain that there was a downside to this jaunt back to Baltimore—beyond the travel expenses and having to wear a dinner jacket and fancy loafers. I would have to be on constant lookout for one odious resident, the esteemed George Hathaway, my uncle. Ours was not a beautiful relationship.

"Uncle George?" I repeated.

Chet rolled his eyes. "*George* Enescu. I was being witty."

I oh-ed happily. It didn't seem all that witty to me, but I was too relieved to criticize. "I thought you meant *my* uncle George. George Hathaway."

It was Chester's turn to flinch. "George Hathaway is your uncle?"

"That's right."

"The congressman?"

I nodded. Congressman George Hathaway. Uncle to me, John Hathaway. I couldn't help speaking nice and slow, to be sure he understood.

Chet went pale. He made his excuses and slithered back to his table. Clearly something about my uncle hadn't set well with our goateed friend. Good old Congressman George. It was the first time I'd ever been glad to be related to the old bastard.

It wasn't long after Chester Callas's mysterious retreat that the speeches began. First up was Nathaniel Goody, the orb-shaped duffer—also, as I had previously suspected, the dean. He wasn't much of a speaker, our Nate. He got lost in his remarks several times and twice held up a pudgy hand in order to indicate our honored guest on his left, realizing afterward that Fleet was standing on his right. The orchestral director Victoria Walters and the sequined woman were the ones on his left. Eventually the ladies faded back into the shadows, and Nate quit trying to use them as PowerPoint slides. He rambled on, and I had another drink.

He did become almost eloquent at one point. For ten minutes he had rambled on about school business, institute business and local businesses business. He now touched on George Enescu and the composer's famous rhapsodies.

"As many of you here know," he said, "there was once rumored to exist a third Romanian Rhapsody in *G* minor."

The audience confirmed this with nods and scholarly whispers. *G* minor, yes. That was what they had always heard.

"This follow-up to Enescu's two masterpieces has been the subject of conjecture in musical circles for decades. Nothing has ever come of it, however, and there have been several false leads since the composer's death, all ending in disappointment. Well, ladies and gentlemen, I am here to tell you that an authentic score has now been discovered."

[Pause for *oohs* and *ahs*]

"I don't have to tell anyone here what this means," he told us, obviously overlooking that I was in the audience. "What it means is—well, it's a triumph; that's what it means. Enescu's 'Romanian Rhapsody Number Three in *G* minor.' How marvelous!"

[Time-out for Nate to ramble on about the triumphant marvel of it all]

"And you, ladies and gentlemen, will be the first to hear it. What could be more fitting for the anniversary of Enescu's birth?" he declared, his sallow features contorting into a smile. "Immediately following the remarks from Mr. Fleet, Mr. Chester Callas, from *Resounding Note* magazine, will perform a transcription on violin. Mr. Callas is the man who discovered the score, so it is only proper that he shall be the first to perform it. And how special will that be!"

[Applause]

I was astounded. Chester had discovered something? I still didn't get what the hoopla was all about, but that a hoopla existed was indisputable.

I peered back, expecting to see that insufferable Callas smirk, but found that Chet and his smirk were no longer present. I figured he had gone to warm up his violin strings, or whatever it is these fiddle players do to get ready.

"And now without further ado—" said Nate Goody.

[Pause for further ado]

"—I give you Enescu Fleet."

[Applause]

I won't leave anyone in suspense. The old rascal gave an excellent speech. We laughed, we cried, we had a marvelous, wondrous time. Beginning with some words of wisdom his Romanian grandmother once told him—it loses something in the translation, he was sorry to say—he segued into what his classical music heritage has meant to him as a private investigator.

My nerves began to unwind. I took a deep breath and smiled at Lesley. I smiled at Ate as well, at the decorative orchid centerpiece, and at a crab cocktail some kindly soul had placed on my plate during the changing of the guard.

I ate (*āt*).

Lesley wrinkled her nose at my choice of fork—all wrong, apparently—but I didn't care. The entire society of forks was beautiful as far as I was concerned. Salad, cocktail, pitch—I loved them all.

Our ordeal was nearly over, and not even the prospect of having to listen to Chester Callas play a transcription of Enescu's third Romanian Rhapsody could dampen my spirits now.

I reached for the *G* and *T*, my fellow undampened spirit, and held the beaker in the air as Fleet brought it on home.

"And that is why the mayor of Bucharest still owes me fifty *lei*," he joked.

The audience burst into laughter.

He stepped out from the podium. "I am reminded of an amusing story about Leo Stokowski…" he observed.

I recognized the cue. We had reached the wrap-up. In tribute to his success—not a single suspicious peep from the gallery—I took my glass and threw back a swig of happy juice.

It was as I was coming down off the follow-through that I noticed a dark, murky object at the bottom of my cocktail. I didn't care for it. I tipped the lip forward, frowning, and discovered that the item was not in my drink at all. It was overhead: a solid, falling object careening toward our table.

I barely had time to yank Lesley and Ate back—some cleavage may well have been unseated in the process—before a human body landed violently on the tablecloth in front of us.

I stared up at Fleet. If this was part of the funny story about Stokowski, I didn't get it.

3 — Resounding End

The gasps and burbles died down. A hush didn't exactly fall over the crowd—in a room as vast as that the echoes alone would last for weeks—but it was a lot less burbly than I would have expected. These modern patrons of the arts know how to take it.

I crept forward and surveyed the snarl. It wasn't difficult to identify: that beefy frame, those priggish lips, the sharply trimmed vandyke (now slightly less neat). Our sudden interloper was none other than Chester Callas.

He didn't look that bad, really. He had a nasty bump on the head, and his silk tuxedo shirt had seen better days, but all in all, he had made a clean landing.

I glanced upward again. Based on his trajectory and the thump with which he hit, I presumed he must have come down from the fourth- or fifth-story balcony. What he was doing up there, and how he managed to take a header over the railing, I couldn't conceive; but here he was. It crossed my mind that he may have been pushed. I remembered thinking something along those lines when we met. The minute he opened his mouth I said to myself, "Now here's a guy who will likely get shoved from a great height someday."

He continued to lay there dazed, chuckling to himself. I was glad he was keeping such a cheerful outlook. I stepped closer, to see if I could fetch him a stretcher or anything, but before I could speak he attached himself to my lapels and reeled me in.

He whispered something to me. I couldn't quite make it out, but he persevered, and eventually I got it. He had landed on my fork. He wanted to know what kind of uncouth baboon used a salad utensil for his appetizer. I had no answer for him.

He brought me in nearer. He whispered two words and laughed lightly.

He expired.

I straightened up to find Enescu Fleet at my side. "Are you alright, Johnny?"

I said I was.

"Is he dead?"

I said if he wasn't, he was doing a marvelous imitation of it.

"Did you see how it happened?"

I said I hadn't. I spoke distractedly. I was still absorbing the dead man's last words, trying to make sense of them. They almost sounded like—no, after all his gibes it hardly seemed likely they could be a clue.

But then again…

I looked over at Ate. She was standing linked arm in arm with my fiancée, both wide-eyed and panting from the shock.

It could have been worse, I supposed. Assuming I was correct and Chester Callas had been shoved, at least he hadn't died holding out four fingers on each hand.

We could scratch off one suspect from the list.

An hour later, we had yet to scratch off another. As a matter of fact, I didn't know if there was a list to scratch anything off of. All I knew for certain was, thanks to Fleet, I had become acquainted with my fifth dead guy in roughly a year. (And one dead guy would have been more than satisfactory.)

On the plus side, the corpse did bring about a snappy close to the evening. Unlike most cultural events I have attended, there was no restless shifting in the seats, no furtive peeks at the time. Just an orderly wrap-up, care of the police. And Fleet didn't have to field any follow-ups on his ancestry. I should have figured it would all work out for him in the end.

By now, the honorable descendent had slid beautifully into his new role, that of lead consulting investigator. No sooner had I begun to siphon the last drop of alcohol from my chalice of ice than I saw him holding court with half the local police force. They had brought him into the fold almost at once. I'd have credited this to the tuxedo, but Fleet could command authority in bathing trunks and a snorkel. He had that kind of personality.

While he commanded, the rest of us tried to make ourselves useful in various ways. I, as previously intimated, drank. Hutton was off on his own somewhere, detecting. From the rumble of official voices overhead, I deduced that he had gone to take an informal gander at the scene of the plunge and found himself formally rebuffed.

He did not have that kind of personality.

Ate, I hadn't seen since the splat. Hopefully, she was busy straightening out our travel arrangements.

Lesley had excused herself during the removal of the body but was back in her seat now, frowning. She was looking as angelic as ever, her chestnut hair hooked behind her earlobe, her cheek as touchably soft as the day we met.

Her eyes, however, told a different story. They were dull, transfixed. It was obvious that the drama of the evening had taken it out of her.

She lifted her head from her hands, and I could tell she was about to take a shy, tentative step toward unburdening herself. "If it weren't for the smidgeon of gore," she said, speaking with remarkable clarity of purpose, "this would be a lovely venue for our wedding reception."

I agreed that it wouldn't be too bad, assuming the management could keep the flying music critics to a minimum. "Wait, you're not seriously considering reserving it, are you?" Her clarity of purpose was beginning to creep me out.

Her big green eyes widened. What I had mistaken for emotional distress was actually the mental acuity of a future bride in need of a knockout reception hall. "No. No, of course not. That would be ghoulish." A short pause. "Still, a guest splayed out across the dinner service should help thin down the queue a bit. I happen to know there's an eighteen-month wait for the space normally." She patted me on the cufflink. "I'll go make a few discreet inquiries, shall I?"

She was halfway across the marble tile before I could open my mouth. Not that it would have mattered. Like Alex Trebek, I was just tickled that she had bothered to phrase her decision in the form of a question.

Hutton immediately flung himself into the seat she had vacated. I would have preferred an entrance a little less vigorous—I'd had enough items landing in my vicinity for one day—but Hutton seldom did what I preferred.

"Prepare to be browbeaten," he snorted.

I swept away the veil of ice his arrival had scattered across my dress shirt and asked for clarification. "Browbeaten by whom?"

"Cops. They're documenting everyone's movements tonight. You'd think they'd never had a journalist bellyflop on a banquet table before. I hate giving official statements, Hath. They always seem to handcuff my future remarks somehow."

"I can see how that would be."

"It took me twenty minutes alone to explain about my name."

I could see how this would be as well. As I believe I've mentioned in previous installments, Hutton wasn't my friend's given name. It wasn't his last name either. Technically speaking, it wasn't his name at all. His real name—well, that's a long story.

I could envision how explaining all this to some faithful public servant, who probably only wished to wrap things up in time to catch the last few innings of the ball game, would be quite the saga.

"Then we got on to my accent," he said. "Is there something curious about my accent, Hath?"

No curiouser than the rest of him, I assured him.

"Exactly. I explained I was British. I pointed out that my time in the States has no doubt chipped the edge off my native drawl a titch, accounting for the mellow twang you hear me speaking today. He seemed unable to accept this."

"You sure it wasn't words like 'titch' he found unacceptable?"

"And somehow," continued Hutton, "this all related to my whereabouts when C. C. took his long walk off a short balcony. And they call this investigating? Is it any wonder that Enescu Fleet made his name famous as a detective in this country? Compared with these incompetent rozzers, Deputy Barney Fife was—well, I don't know what, actually; but these guys stink."

A blistering harangue, to be sure, but I let it pass. One of his earlier comments had penetrated my consciousness. "Where were you anyway?"

"How's that?"

"Where were you during Fleet's speech?

It suddenly struck me that he hadn't been in his seat when Chet took his spill. There were plates, stemware, the fancy orchid trimmings and my fork, all sailing off in every direction, but no Hutton. I could only conclude that he had been somewhere else.

"Where was I?" he asked.

"Yes," I replied. "Where were you?"

According to Hutton, if I squinted when I said that and had a good deal more pastrami on my breath, I would be the spitting image of his recent inquisitor.

"You don't seriously believe me capable—"

I said of course I didn't. I seldom believed he was capable. "I'm just curious."

"Ah. Well, the fact is, I went for a walk."

"A walk?"

"It's done by moving one leg in front of the other—"

"I'm familiar. But why walk during Fleet's speech?"

"I wasn't in the mood. I needed air." It wasn't one of his best explanations.

He took off his glasses and polished them on a flap of the tablecloth. The horn-rims were new, part of his ongoing practice to swap out his eyewear every year or so. The polish, on the other hand, was old. I recognized it right off. It was a pensive polish, the polish of a man with a troubled soul.

He popped the frames back in place and scowled. For the second time that night, I felt certain one of my circle was about to unship some pretty hefty emotion. He let me have it. "Have you seen those little crab-puff thingies floating around here anywhere?" he asked.

"Crab-puff thingies?" I repeated.

"Pastry doodads, filled with crab. They were whisking them about on silver platters before the speeches started."

I said no, I hadn't seen any silver-plattered finger food. I hadn't noticed any food at all, in fact, not since a tall, well-fed male nearly squashed me and my fiancée in our seats.

"Ah," said Hutton. "Well, they have to be lurking about somewhere," he argued. And with these weighty words, he got up and left.

As he ankled off, I could see a mustached man with a sandpaper complexion waving me over to a distant book grotto. Time to go make my official statement to the police, I gathered.

It was just as well. I had important things to do; Hutton had important things to do. It was all good.

Never let it be said that John Hathaway would come between a man and his puffs.

4 — The Man and his Musings

The officer had a few things to ask before I signed off on my sworn statement. They were fairly typical questions. *How well did I know the deceased?* I didn't. *Had I seen him speaking with anyone else this evening?* I hadn't. *Could I think of anyone who might have wanted to do Chester Callas harm?* I couldn't (which is to say, I could, but *Anyone who has ever met him* was hardly the answer he was going for).

I was beginning to detect a certain trend in the officer's inquiry. It was subtle, but I'm good at picking up on subtleties. "Then it wasn't an accident?"

The detective made no reply.

"Not death by misadventure?" I asked, amazing the man with my knowledge of the lingo. I was fairly certain that was the lingo.

He gave a curt frown. "We're treating this as a murder investigation," he muttered, and I responded with a sharp *ha!* of gratification. Death by non-misadventure. Exactly as I had suspected.

I probably could have laid off the smug satisfaction a titch. It wasn't winning me any points with the constabulary.

"You seem pleased," he said.

I hastened to justify my *ha*—and quick. You can't go around snickering like a B-movie master villain and not raise a few eyebrows. This was a murder investigation, after all.

"Not so much pleased as vindicated," I explained. "Or self-vindicated, if that's a thing. I thought there might be some horseplay with this accident, you see, and some horseplay there has proven to be. That's where the vindication comes in. You know how it is when you make a bet with yourself that something is one way, when it could be another way altogether, and then you find out that it was the first way after all, and you think to yourself *ha*, I won?"

"No."

"Right," I said. No reason why he should. "Anyway, that's why I said ha."

The cop made a clicking sound between his mustached lips, suggesting he had something stuck in his teeth. Pastrami perhaps. "You're British?" he asked.

"A common misconception," I told him. "I'm American. Born in the US, bred in the UK."

"Yeah?"

"I wouldn't kid you. It's the old story: congressman uncle, made guardian of a nephew he couldn't stand the sight of, ships nephew off to boarding school in England at a young age. Nephew arrives home a decade later, meets and becomes engaged to a girl, who, as happenstance would have it, is English herself. You know the sort of thing?"

Oddly enough, he didn't. "You sound British," he said.

I didn't deny it. Between my schooling and the future Mrs. Hathaway, my speech had developed something of an Anglo-American flair. A mellow twang, if you like.

Naturally, there were downsides to this. "I can never decide whether to spell *color* with a 'u' or not," I quipped.

I flashed him another of my Anglo-American smiles, and he went back to his lip chirping.

"England is where you first met the deceased?"

"That's right."

"You were friends?"

"Not especially," I replied, not wishing to speak ill of the dead. As tactfully as I could, I made it clear that Chester Callas was not the sort of man I would have called a friend.

The officer understood. He jotted down a few notes. "Is that 'dick-weed' with a hyphen?" he wondered.

I said I thought it had a hyphen, yes, but he shouldn't quote me on it.

"And what was the nature of your conversation tonight?" he inquired.

"Just picking up old threads. What there were of them. He actually came over to speak with another mutual friend of ours. Hutton. You've met him, I believe."

The officer said yes. They'd met. He paged back through his notes. "And what about after the fall? Did the deceased say anything to you?"

In a real, technical sense, a deceased wouldn't say anything at all. I caught his drift, however. "He did whisper something, now that you mention it."

"And what was that?"

"Oh, just something about forks."

"You mean like tuning forks?"

I smiled. The musical motif. The officer had done his homework. "No, an actual fork," I said. "He seemed unhappy about it. We talked about that for a while."

"And after that?"

"After that," I repeated. "After that…" I said again, gazing across the library at Hutton.

The London Twang was talking up a storm with a female member of the Pendleton catering staff. They appeared to be probing into the whole Missing Crab-Puff Mystery.

"What did he say after that…?" I pondered aloud.

Still, I hesitated. I was playing a dangerous game here, I realized, holding back information from the police; but until I knew more about Hutton's movements and motivations, I felt a few games were worth the risk.

"It's hard to say," I concluded. "I mentioned the fork, yes? Let's see. Fork, dislike of fork, death. No, that's about all I can remember."

Fortunately, before we could hash out Chet's post-fork remarks any further, Enescu Fleet sailed in to the rescue. He wanted to know if he could take me off the officer's hands for a moment. There was something he could use my assistance with upstairs.

Except for those times when he's embellishing his backstory or foisting aliases off on me against my will (a favorite pastime of his), I have always enjoyed assisting Fleet with his cases. I don't know how much help I am, really, but he seems to appreciate having me around. I think he likes having someone to bounce ideas off of.

Just for tonight, I would have been glad to have kept this bouncing in check. We were way too far up in the atmosphere to risk some bold assertion knocking one of us over the banisters.

The site of Chester Callas's last bow occurred on the fifth-story balcony, about halfway down the line in a section focused on sports medicine. If only he had bothered to slip a slim volume off the shelves relating to the dangers of bungee-cord jumping without a cord, a lot of stress could have been avoided here.

We reached the locale, and I took a cursory sweep of the surroundings.

Nothing appeared to be out of the ordinary. If there had been a struggle, the participants must have prided themselves on a rapid and orderly cleanup.

I took a peek over the railing and soon wished I hadn't. I don't usually suffer from vertigo, but it occurred to me that the sight of all those tiny tables and chairs, set against a sea of black-and-white marble, was something only Kim Novak could have viewed with any kind of pleasure. The whole landscape swam before my eyes—the tiny officers of the law collecting tiny statements from tiny remaining guests—and then, with the help of Fleet, I pulled back.

"High," I commented.

Fleet conceded that there were less tall libraries.

I took another step away from the precipice. "It's no wonder Chester Callas checked out after riding this ride. I'm amazed he could speak. Which reminds me, what makes them think it was murder? Did someone see him shoved?"

Fleet shook his head. "Nobody seems to have seen anything."

"Then how do they know he didn't slip?"

"They're not certain the fall killed him."

This was crazy. An entire room of people saw the fall kill him.

"You misunderstand me. The medical examiner isn't convinced that the fall was the cause of death. Chester was stabbed."

I sighed. "Look, I'm sorry I left my salad fork lying on the table—"

"It wasn't your fork, Johnny. Somebody stabbed Chester Callas in the shoulder with a penknife. You probably didn't notice because his long hair covered the wound."

I was shocked. "So he was stabbed and *then* shoved over the rail? Amazing."

Fleet agreed that it had its amazing side.

"Whose fingerprints were on the knife?"

"That's still up in the air. At this point, the only prints the authorities can identify for certain are Chester's himself." He paused. "Speaking of things up in the air," he said, "I've been meaning to ask: what did he say to you after he fell?"

I hesitated no longer. The cops were one thing, but this was Enescu Fleet. The Fleets could be trusted.

"It didn't make any sense," I replied.

"Let's have it anyway."

"It was a name."

"What sort of name?"

"*Frank Sinatra,*" I said. That sort of name.

5 — Lively Number

"Frank Sinatra?" asked Enescu Fleet.

I confirmed this. Sinatra, Frank. Those were Chester Callas's last words. "The name seemed to amuse him, as if speaking it had given him the giggle of a lifetime."

"I suppose, in a way, it did," answered my distinguished friend, leaning the small of his back against the railing.

A few minutes passed, and I decided to up the ante on my two cents. I wasn't sure if this would technically come under the heading of idea-bouncing, but even walls yearn to speak up occasionally. "I've been giving it some thought, and I think it all relates back to the visit he made to our table before your speech."

Here, I gave Fleet a quick rundown of Chet's social call: his barbs about Ate's name, his scorn of our previous cases, and his views on whether a murder victim would possess the wherewithal to leave behind a clue to his own murder.

"In short, if I were to translate that giggle into plain English, it would be, *Ha, after all my sneering, here I am leaving a clue of my own. Ha-ha.* Or," I added, offering a different shade of meaning, "it could have been, *Ha, you like dying clues so much, do you? Well, try this one on for size, ha-ha.*"

Fleet nodded. "So you would say the 'ha-ing' was essential either way?"

I felt it was.

"And you feel Frank Sinatra is a clue?"

"I do."

"So do I," he replied.

He moved away from the railing, his bow tie dangling from his open collar. It was a good look: aging Rat Pack.

"I want you to see something," he said, nodding to an item behind me.

I turned. I saw.

"The phone on the wall," he indicated. "What do you think?"

I thought it looked like a phone. Beige, wired—an old phone.

"They have a unit on every level throughout the library," he explained.

"Very progressive."

"The idea was, if you had to ask the librarian something, you didn't have to hoof it down five flights of stairs to locate her."

"Ingenious," I said.

"They've been more or less replaced by cell phones now, but the line still works, and I gather that some visitors still make use of them."

I suppose my only response to this was "Awesome," with as little topspin on the remark as I could manage (I didn't want to batter the old guy's feelings too badly). I opened my mouth.

"Chester's fingerprints were all over it," he said.

I closed my mouth. I was beginning to view the antique in a whole new light.

So Chet had snuck away from his table in order to make (or receive) a clandestine call? A call, which for some reason, he didn't wish to receive (or make) on his mobile. Interesting—not to mention awesome.

"Do they know who he called, or who called him?"

"They're checking on it for me. We can be reasonably confident that the call came in and not out. His fingerprints were found on the receiver, not the keypad."

I nodded. It was possible, of course, that he had wiped down each key with an itty-bitty handkerchief, just to throw us off, but I considered this unlikely. "So now we wait?"

The master PI had a better idea. "I was wondering how you would feel about nipping down to another extension and giving this one a buzz."

"Giving it a buzz?"

"So I can see how it works."

"Nipping?" I asked.

"Or however you see fit to proceed," he replied.

So that was it, was it? That was why he had drawn me away from the police, just when Detective Sergeant Mustache and I were getting along so well.

He needed a runner.

I don't mind telling you, the suggestion rankled. I was used to playing Watson to his Holmes, but I resented playing Watson to his Bell.

"Can't we just assume the thing goes *tingle-ling* and you talk into one end and listen at the other?"

"Johnny—"

"I mean, I can try it right now on my mobile, if you like." I withdrew my iPhone from my pocket and twirled it invitingly.

It was no good. These were internal lines; they would only accept calls from phones on the campus switchboard. The wusses.

"Johnny, this could be significant."

Well, as long as he put it that way…

Ask around, and I bet you'll find most people know about the Pendleton Library. It's pretty world renowned. What with all its fancy functions and scholarly texts, it's a landmark most people have at least heard of.

That's terrific—I'm happy for them—but I'm here to say most people don't know Jack Stokowski about the Pendleton. Students, researchers, banquet guests—all amateurs. Until you have run up and down its five flights of stairs in slippery dress loafers, you don't know the Pendleton the way I know the Pendleton.

It didn't help that I had to go up and down twice—once because I had forgotten to ask the extension on the damned alcove phone, and another because I couldn't remember the extension on the damned alcove phone.

Eventually I got it straight, and after a prolonged discussion with a Pendleton librarian about running on the steps, and a longer discussion assuring her that I was not borrowing her landline to ring up Bucharest, I made my call.

After several rings, Fleet answered suavely: "Hello?"

"It's me."

"Johnny?"

I hoofed an impatient loafer. The librarian told me no dancing in her alcove.

"Are we done here?" I asked.

My tormentor agreed that we were. "Come up here, Johnny—I want to see you."

I rang off and returned to the spot of our great experiment in the sky. I was out of breath and had a blister on my foot, but I was there. "Well?"

Fleet filled me in. "There was no ring. Just a flashing light."

Made sense. It was a library, after all.

"See this tiny LED screen here?"

I saw it.

"It displays the extension calling in."

I could have told him that. What else did he think tiny LED screens were for? "That was why you had me running up and down the stairs?"

"More or less."

"And was it significant?"

He couldn't say. Could be. Could not be. We'd have to chew on it.

Hearing him describe it that way, I realized that I could use something to chew on myself. I was starving. And exhausted.

His chiseled features softened. He could see that his faithful legman was not his typical oxygen-rich self. "You're out of breath, Johnny."

I wheezed that I was aware of that. Running sprints all evening will have that effect.

"I was wondering about that. Why'd you go all the way down the steps? I told you there was a phone on every level. You could have used the one right below us."

I wheezed out a reply, unfit for such distinguished company, and we hit the stairs again.

6 — The Chairman of the Board

I wasn't too tuckered out to brood on the case as we descended. From where I had been sitting, virtually anyone could have done in Chester during the speeches. It was dark, the audience had been speech-riveted, and if the man's party persona was any indicator, the motives for pushing him to his death (and/or stabbing him in the shoulder) would have been boundless. It gave me food for thought.

This was more than I could say for the Pendleton kitchen. I guess when you have police whizzing about everywhere, taking statements and fielding Q & A, presenting the attractively plated morsels takes a backseat.

Nevertheless, I felt a truly dedicated catering corps would have found a way. I didn't even see any signs of Hutton's crab-puffs.

What I did see was the less bulbous duffer from the speaking platform: the man who had deferred to Nate Goody in the matter of rousing opening speeches.

I didn't know who he was, but he seemed a mellow enough geezer: average height and build, sagging jowls, widow's peak the color and texture of damp pillow fluff. Now, *he* looked sedate and unadventurous.

Fleet introduced us. "John Hathaway, Lyle Pendleton."

Lyle looked less than thrilled. We shook hands, but you could tell he would have just as soon yawned in my face.

"Pendleton?" I asked.

"Lyle is the last of the fabulous Pendletons," Fleet answered, where Lyle refused.

"No kidding?"

"He's a sort of consultant now. Evaluates policy, acts as trustee. He's the chairman of the board, in fact."

I stood there, staring dumbly. In the words of Chester Callas, I was all keyed up.

Lyle Pendleton was the chairman. The Chairman of the Board. I knew of another man who once favored that honorific: an old songster by the name of Francis Albert Sinatra.

In a haze, I followed the men over to a lounge at the back of the library. There were leather seats here and a fireplace and an ornate wood mantel brimming over with carved elks and antelopes and things. I didn't pay these much attention. My thoughts were riveted elsewhere.

They took a couple of seats, leaving me to linger beside the antelopes and elks. I missed most of the conversation. Fleet had asked Pendleton something about the phones in the library, what system they were on and how records were kept, and Pendleton had confessed that the library phones were a sealed book to him. The man we should see on that was Nathaniel Goody. He had supervised the installation decades ago. If we wanted the straight dope on how they worked, Nate was our guy, said the Chairman.

Or words to that effect.

I came out of my fog to see Lyle Pendleton cupping his fleecy head in his hands. He wouldn't have expected things to go down this way, he muttered. "Chester Callas. It doesn't make sense. Where does the Brit come into it?"

Fleet couldn't tell him, but he could be certain, Lyle could, that he would find the answer (Fleet would).

Pendleton stood. "We shouldn't be talking here. Come by my house later?"

Fleet said he'd be delighted to drop in. So to speak. Pendleton thanked him with a nod, threw a scowl my way, and left.

Fleet took a position beside me at the mantel. I must have been staring at Pendleton's empty chair, because the sudden presence at my elbow caused me to jump. "What?"

"I said you seem perturbed."

"Do I?"

"Even the carved antelope could tell you were agitated. What's going on?"

I told him I was agitated, and possibly a little perturbed. "Didn't you hear yourself earlier?"

He nodded. He always heard himself. He had a wonderful speaking voice.

"Lyle is the chairman," I uttered.

"Yes?"

"The Chairman of the Board."

"Oh that." He smiled. "That amused me as well."

"Amused you!"

"Should it not have?"

My feet did another restless soft-shoe on the throw rug. The Library Guardian, striding past at that moment, told me no tap-dancing in the lounges.

I pressed my point with Fleet: "You asked for something significant. It doesn't get much more significant than this!"

He sat on the arm of the chair. "You suspect Lyle Pendleton?"

Of course I suspected Lyle! Who wouldn't suspect Lyle? "He freely admits that he's the chairman of the board, on the very evening that a dying man spouts the name of Frank Sinatra, the most chairman of the board Chairman of the Board of them all. It seems to me that the case is solved and in record time."

"Is it?"

"Of course. If we hurry, we might be able to slap the cuffs on the killer and be back at our hotel for a late snack." Not only that, but I had overheard someone saying the ball game had gone into extras. We could still catch the bottom of the 14th.

Fleet thought all that sounded grand. If I didn't mind, though, he would like to go on with his investigations a while longer.

"Back when I was a full-time private eye, I never liked to stand pat on the first suspect that came my way. I preferred to question everyone involved, assemble motives and opportunities. In short, bill for the entire hour."

I frowned. I thought he was passing up on a good thing—how many Sinatra references were we going to get?—but I understood. He was being thorough.

As for the snack, I could stand it if he could. If malnourishment settled in, I could always fall back on the old Life Saver I found in my tuxedo earlier. That was all peachy—the situation not the candy—but there was something I still didn't get.

"You don't suspect Lyle Pendleton at all?"

"Let's just say I have my reasons not to suspect him," said Fleet. "But I appreciate the effort, Johnny. We'll hold that one in our back pocket for now," he remarked, and thumped me warmly on the padded shoulder.

I sniffed. Most people would have found his words (and thump) patronizing. But when you've been steeped in British understatement most of your life as I have, Fleet's brand of hearty American condescension goes down a lot smoother. Like the Life Saver, you take what you can get.

"So where do we go now?" I asked.

"Where all hot-blooded rogues wind up eventually," he replied. "The dean's office."

I said oh Goody. The round duffer.

We discovered the round one in his lair, looking circular and jittery and not at all the jovial podium-rambler of a few hours back. Dean Nathaniel Goody was not himself.

His office was nice and plush, although there was also a touch of the timeworn about it. It clearly hadn't been decorated since the early sixties—or whenever brown, yellow and moss last dominated the designer's palette. It smelled of must and social unrest.

The dean was sitting behind a giant mahogany desk, gazing out through giant, square glasses. What he had zoned in on I couldn't determine, but it might have been a cobweb, or perhaps he had only now noticed all the browns, yellows and mosses.

His secretary offered us a brandy as we came in. Something to calm our nerves. I was pretty full of gin already, but if the drink was to be in service of nerve-calming, I thought I should probably have a go at it. A double, if it was convenient.

Nate's cohorts from the assembly had joined us. Seated on a sofa of orange and gold, and what looked like some kind of cushion made of animal hair, I observed the music director, Victoria Walters, ensconced alongside the lady in sequins.

This, it turned out, was Tanya Saxon, the grande dame of Pendleton. She had to be about ninety, or possibly a youthful hundred.

According to Fleet, and if anyone would know, it was he, Tanya had done it all. In her prime she had deaned, directed and endowed. If she ever passed on, her ghost would presumably preside over the Institute as a beacon of old-world excellence. Until then, the resident elder contented herself with lending the place a commanding confidence and no-nonsense aplomb you could feel in the next county.

She seemed nice.

Victoria, I warmed to more readily. She, too, had not made herself idle in her forty odd years. Going by the article I had read earlier, she was a respected cellist and violinist; she sang, both choral and jazz; and even composed. But it was in orchestral directing that her talents best lay. I had heard some scuttlebutt around the banquet hall that her kindly exterior masked a ruthless soul, bent on success no matter what, but I didn't buy it. I knew geniality when I saw it, and she was plenty genial. She reminded me of Billie Holiday or someone.

I think it was her eyes that set me most at ease. You don't come across many African American women with peepers the color of bold sapphires, but that's what hers were. Add a pleasant, apple-shaped face and a soothing smile, and she would have been my choice for orchestra director, easy. I could see the lowliest hornist coming to her with hiccups an hour before the big concert, and her bucking the poor player up in no time at all. She struck me as a good sort.

Coming more fully into the room, I sipped my beverage and waited for someone to say something. There were no takers.

While we waited, I found myself drawn once more to those eyes of Victoria's. They were most unusual.

Victoria's blue eyes. Blue eyes. Ol' Blue—

I spilled my double brandy.

7 — Ol' Blue Eyes

In truth, she wasn't that old—or *ol'*. But her eyes were undeniably blue, as blue as a certain eminent crooner's.

Everywhere you looked, we were getting plinked by Sinatra nicknames.

I pondered hard, putting myself in Chester's place. If I had recently been stabbed in the shoulder with a penknife and shoved over a fifth-story railing at a fancy banquet, what would I have latched onto in my mind? Might it have been the unusual eye color of my killer? Could that have stuck in my noodle as I plummeted headlong toward the upper crust? And assuming that color was firmly planted in my head, mightn't I have later burbled out the first thing that wandered in from my battered subconscious (i. e., the name of that celebrated blue-eyed one—Ol' Blue Eyes himself)?

Could be, I thought, could be.

Victoria was staring up at me from the sofa. "Is everything okay?" she asked.

I said sure, never better. Why did she ask?

"It's just your brandy…my dress…"

She indicated the garment, also blue (and now brandy soaked), and I said something burbling and apologetic.

She waved it off. "It's fine. I just wanted to make sure you weren't having a fit or anything."

I attempted to wave this off myself, but only ended up sloshing the goblet again. "Does brandy stain silk?" I asked the room. No one answered.

"Come, my dear," said Tanya Saxon, rising to the rescue. "We'll see what a dab of club soda will do."

The ladies left.

Fortunately, the men didn't give me too hard a time. You know how guys can be, always ready to rag on the slightest bout of clumsiness in their fellow males. I got a pass that night. Aside from a word about cutting Johnny off, Fleet said nothing, and Nate was too absorbed in his own thoughts to offer any recriminations. The whiff of alcohol in the air did remind him that he had an excellent Romanian *tuica* around here somewhere, if we cared to partake of it.

"Now where did my secretary, Mrs. Drake, stash the case?"

Fleet suggested that we shelve the tuica for the nonce.

Nate looked up. Shelf. Maybe she had slid a bottle behind one of the books on his shelf. He stood to search for it. Fleet waved him off. "Rough business tonight, Nate."

The dean heaved a sigh. The roughest, he agreed, returning to his chair. "And on the night honoring your ancestor, George Enescu." He rattled his large head.

Fleet said that he and his ancestor would get over it. "You mentioned a third Romanian Rhapsody during your speech?"

Nate leaned forward. His chair made a squawk. "Oh yes. Yes. A wonderful find. I couldn't believe it when I saw the score."

"May we take a look at it?"

Nate said absolutely, absolutely. "It's much longer than what Callas would have played. He adapted a small portion into a transcription for solo violin. Now which drawer was it in?" he wondered, pulling this handle, then that.

His phone buzzed on his desk. *"Dr. Goody—?"*

"Not now, Mrs. Drake!"

"Dr. Goody, several members of the board have arrived. Dr. Pendleton was hoping you could spare them a moment."

"Yes, yes, yes," said Nate irritably, nearly slamming his thumb in one of his cabinets. "Mrs. Drake?"

"Yes, Dr. Goody?"

"Did you see a purple folder on my desk yesterday?"

"Yes, Dr. Goody."

"Do you know where it is now?"

"No, Dr. Goody."

"Damn!" This time he did catch his thumb. He sucked on it. "Musses Deke?"

"Yes, Dr. Goody?"

"Hap you seem my tuica?"

"No, Dr. Goody."

Nate said *dwam*. The line went dead.

"I must have put the rhapsody score in the safe," he said, heading for the assembly of photos on the wall. He removed a sepia pic of Lyle Pendleton and himself holding a marlin.

He began twirling the dial.

Fleet was looking at the phone on the desk, the handset lying half-off the hook where the dean had flung it. "I wanted to ask you, Nate, would it be possible to get a log of internal calls placed tonight?"

"Internal calls?"

"Calls placed internally."

The dean grumbled something under his breath, puffed on his fingertips, and started his twirling again. "What was that? No, sorry. The police asked about that too. It's an old system. There aren't any logs when a call is from one extension to another."

He finally got the safe door open. Only eight tries. Not bad.

He started pawing through the papers inside.

"You understand the score I have is only a copy," he explained. "Callas had the original."

A few more minutes of rifling and he stepped back from the hole, blinking. He turned and stared blankly at us, much the way I had stared upon learning that Lyle Pendleton was the chairman of the board.

"It's not here."

Fleet glanced past him. "Not in your safe?"

"Not anywhere," said Nate Goody, as blank as ever.

8 — Hathaway in G Major

We left Nate Goody to his board meeting. As we filed out, he insisted that he would find the missing score around here somewhere. It only required a little digging. (Of course, that's what he had said about the tuica.)

I must have been brooding again, or at least plucking at the fibers of my tux too much, because Fleet gripped my shoulder in the hallway outside Mrs. Drake's desk and asked me why I was looking like a maître d' who had just seated the governor's wife next to his mistress.

"What's on your mind, Johnny? You're not still mulling on Lyle Pendleton, are you?"

Actually, I had never ceased mulling on Lyle. The Chairman remained excellent mulling fodder in my mind. But no, I wasn't focused on Lyle. As much as I loathed to consider it, my mull had settled on a new candidate for murderer. I was about to share these unwelcome thoughts when the candidate herself poked her head out from the doorway.

Apparently all the high-ups had an office in this corridor.

"Mr. Fleet, do you have a moment?" asked Victoria Walters. She appeared comparably brandy-free now.

Fleet assured her that he had plenty, all at her disposal, and asked her to call him Ef, pronounced like the letter *F*. They disappeared together into her office, and the door shut. I guess I wasn't invited.

It was of no consequence. I make my own fun.

As a matter of fact, I spotted some fun that very instant. I should mention that the hallway I was in tailed off at a cherrywood staircase. Beneath this staircase was a sort of junior vestibule, nowhere near as grand as the main lobby but posh in its way and handy if you were looking to make an exit without a lot of fanfare. I bring this up because, while I leaned against the polished balustrade, counting floor tiles, a shadowy figure scuttled across this tiny foyer, with just such an unheralded exit in mind.

I stiffened. I recognized this scuttling, shadowy figure. I recognized the hell out of it. What it was doing in the shadows—and why it scuttled—I intended to find out.

I skipped down the steps, nearly taking a header in my soft-soled loafers, and stalked up behind him.

The figure was furtive, no question about it. Dressed in the customary tuxedo, only more battle worn, it stooped below the door, peering out into the night in the manner of a wealthy fawn about to shoot shyly across a two-lane blacktop.

I crept closer. "Uncle George?"

The figure sprang up, spun around and goggled. "Johnny!"

Well, that's who I was. No question about that either.

"What are you doing?" I asked.

He slid back from the window and swept a hand over his expansive brow.

"Johnny. I'm glad to see you."

I had made an error. This couldn't be my Uncle George. The congressman and I are never glad to see each other. It's one of the few things we agree on. That, and the fact that the happiest moment of our combined lives was the day he shipped me off to boarding school in England, twenty years ago.

"I need your help," spoke this compelling pod-person.

I was astonished, absolutely astonished. This went beyond the theory of extraterrestrials inhabiting Congress. Uncle George wanted my help. He wasn't ordering me to help; he wasn't tricking me into helping. He was *requesting* it.

"Are you hiding?"

He had finished with his brow-mopping. He now moved on to his tuxedo lapels. He kept smoothing them, up then down, down then up. They looked fine to me.

"I need a way out of here without anyone seeing me."

I strolled away from the door. I resisted the urge to tug on his Uncle George disguise. If some enterprising alien life-form had gone to the trouble to fashion an intricate Hathaway facade, I saw no sense in mucking up its handiwork.

"Why?" I asked.

He went back to his brow, then to his lapels, then a combination of both. Kids who could rub their tummies and tap their heads at the same time had nothing on him.

"I'm trying to avoid the press," he explained.

I nodded. Seemed sensible.

"In order to do that, I'm afraid I've had to steer clear of the authorities in the performance of their duties this evening."

He had come to the right place. In years past, I, too, had been compelled to give the thin blue line a wide margin. "You want to know how to stay one step ahead of the law?"

"I wouldn't exactly put it that way, no."

No. That would mean he was some sort of criminal, rather than a simple congressman. A subtle distinction, I agree, but worth observing.

I paused, staring suddenly.

"What?" asked Uncle George. My sudden stare was freaking him out.

"Nothing," I remarked, "nothing."

It was not nothing. It was his visage. I had never noticed before how much my one-time guardian resembled Frank Sinatra. I'm talking ancient Frank here, you understand: the melon-shaped head, the piercing glare, the fireplug physique. Congressman Hathaway could have been his modern-day doppelgänger. I know it sounds incredible. It might well have been that I was developing some kind of Sinatra complex, a reaction to all the tuxedo lint perhaps. I don't know. But that's how he looked.

Good ol' Frank. It was the dying clue that kept on living.

"So did you do it?" I sighed.

And just like that, the intimidation I had always felt around this relative evaporated.

I had felt a modicum of this liberation years ago when I came into my own money, rendering me financially independent of the old skinflint. That feeling had swelled slightly when I brought Lesley into one of his sessions to introduce them. That had been fun; my fiancée is very dishy, and she certainly made a splash among our other elected officials; but the satisfaction hadn't lasted (although to this day she continues to receive many nice offers to intern).

This was different. Better.

My question seemed to throw him. "Do it? Do what?"

"Kill Chester Callas." I wondered if he had started pricing alibis yet. Probably had. These politicians usually have the right people on speed dial.

"Kill—I didn't kill anyone!" he rasped. "I'd never—unless you have forgotten, I am a member of the US House of Representatives."

I hadn't forgotten. And he had a point. I apologized. "Did you *hire* someone to kill him?" I asked.

The flame in his expression faded. He put his hand on my arm. "I swear to you, I had nothing to do with the accident tonight."

"The murder you mean."

"Was it murder?"

It was. If he had spoken with the police like a good boy, he would have known that.

He pulled away. "This is ridiculous. I didn't even know the man. I'm only here because I get these invitations and it looks good to rub elbows with the artsy set."

"He knew you," I said.

"What?"

"I mentioned you to Chet before dinner, and he knew you like nobody's business. There was no mistaking the look of horror in his eyes."

My uncle refused to bandy words. He maintained that they had never met. The fact that people may have heard of him was utterly irrelevant. Need he not remind me that as a member of the US House of Representatives, he was a well-known public figure.

I sniffed. He was a well-known something.

"The press are crawling around here everywhere, Johnny. I can't afford this kind of negativity in my campaign right now. It's an election year."

"Is it?"

"It's always an election year," he grumbled. He swatted peevishly at a mosquito. Guess he didn't need its vote.

"My opponents would eat this up. I can't be found at a murder scene, not now. Already one of them has an ad implying that I consort with the criminal underworld."

"You do consort with the criminal underworld," I retorted.

He gripped my arm again. All this physicality. And this from a man who didn't even shake my hand until I was twenty-three.

"Your friend, the detective—perhaps he can pull some strings…"

I shook my head. I was aware that this was how things worked in the world of politics, but Enescu Fleet could not be bought.

George scowled. "I meant that other detective you associate with. Your contemporary."

"Hutton?"

"Yes. Hutton." He sang out the name so joyously that you would have thought they were the best of friends.

If they were, my uncle might want to quit calling him *that Limey psychopath*, his invariable phrase for Hutton ever since the latter tagged home with me one winter vacation fifteen years ago. "Hutton," he declared. "I saw him earlier, and he looked as wonderfully devious as ever. Let's ask him what he can do."

I hated to burst the old man's bubble, but Hutton had his own problems with the cops. Detective or not, he was in no position to render assistance to another popular suspect. "Wait, you saw him?"

"Just before I heard the screams. He was walking around the lobby with his head down. I strode past him, but he didn't look up."

This altered everything. So Hutton had been telling the truth. He *had* gone for a walk, not slinked off to satisfy his bloodlust by stabbing and shoving our old classmate. Not that I ever doubted him. But it was nice to have confirmation.

"Let's say your story stands up, Uncle George. What do you need me for?"

He drew me back to the door. He pointed to a murky form outside. "No one leaves without getting past the checkpoint," whispered my uncle. "There were some uniforms milling around before, and Channel 13 News was here too. But I think now it's just this officer. For all I know he could be here for the duration."

I nodded sympathetically. We could all benefit from term limits.

"Tell me, Johnny, you wouldn't want to sneak up behind this man—perhaps apply some of those expensive judo lessons I paid for when you were a child—"

No, I wouldn't want to do that. And they weren't that expensive. And it was aikido.

"I might be able to do something," I said. "Wait here."

I've never found it all that difficult keeping the cops distracted. They seem to find my persona impossible to resist. They drink me in and study my every facial twitch. I must remind them of a test subject they encounter in detective school.

I reached the form, and picture my delight when I beheld my friend from the inquisition: Sergeant Detective Lip Hair. "Oh hi."

The officer took a puff from his cigarette. "Sir."

A pleasant August breeze played about our faces: mine clean-shaven, his weighed down with mustaches and deep thoughts. Somewhere an owl hooted.

"Having a cig?" I said, wowing the man anew with my investigative prowess.

He sniffed. He removed the object from his lips, expelled smoke and asked, reluctantly, if I would like one.

I shook my head. I didn't smoke. Filthy habit.

"Can I show you something instead?"

"Show me what?" he wanted to know.

"Might be easier if you saw it."

I led him away from the door. The library building was at the edge of the campus. We were in the city now.

"Well?" he asked.

It wasn't a bad question. I looked, listened and pondered. Then I had it. "I think I saw a cufflink lying here earlier. Someone must have lost it."

"So?"

"So, I figured it could be a clue."

"And what makes you think that?"

I told him that I had merely assumed. "I mean, a lost cufflink, left at the scene of the murder, always seems to factor into these black-tie crimes eventually. Or an earring. An earring or cufflink, depending on sex."

I raised my head. He was wearing that official gaze I knew so well.

"Why didn't you pick it up when you saw it?"

Now this was surprising. "I didn't like to tamper with evidence. What if it had fingerprints or DNA or splattered blood on it? What then?"

"But you say you saw it before the murder?"

"That's true. Maybe not blood, then."

"And we haven't heard anything about a missing cufflink factoring into the case."

"No? Well, it looks like the culprit retrieved it anyway," I said, peering back at Uncle George's door. "Guess we'll just have to let it go for now."

I took my leave. If that didn't give the congressman time enough to scurry around the corner then I gave up. He could become the Phantom of the Pendleton for all I cared.

I returned to the vestibule and found it empty of uncles of any description. The relative had scurried well. Good for him. His political training had not been for naught.

I headed for the stairs. I was tired, hungry, and twice now I had interfered with the police in the performance of their duties. It had been a full day.

I don't know what made me peer up just then. A remembrance of falling bodies perhaps. Whatever the reason, I did (peer up) and suddenly found myself locking eyes with a shady individual leaning over the rail above me. I couldn't get a good look at his face, but I got a sense of him. Athletic yet refined. Deadly. At least that was the feeling he instilled. It was his stare mostly: dark, homicidal, but not blue-eyed—that was something, I suppose.

And then he was gone. By the time I arrived on the top step there was no trace of him. Not even a dropped cufflink.

9 — Inadequate Arrangement

The shady figure wasn't the only one to absent himself from the scene. Enescu Fleet had also vanished, as had Victoria Walters. The office of the director of the orchestra was empty.

I determined this by sticking my face in the doorway and peering around. I tried knocking first, but this merely caused the latch to slip free from the plate and the door to creak open. If I hadn't already experienced enough flights of fancy for one evening, I might have concluded that someone had been tampering with the lock.

I continued to inspect the interior. I wouldn't technically call this breaking and entering. I'd call it creaking and peering—a totally different matter. I believe my friend, the police sergeant, would support this.

Once you have creaked and peered, you might as well cross the threshold. It's a natural progression. (You can see how infamous cat burglars get started.) I stepped inside and continued my survey from within.

The office of the director was more compact than the dean's, but it had it all over Nate's in decor. Victoria's space was bright and modern, with an admirable sense of organization. I guess you don't become orchestral director at an elite music college without demonstrating that you can keep your knickknacks in harmony.

There was one item out of place, however. On the rug beneath her chair I spotted a loose pamphlet. It leapt to my attention immediately. Women who arrange their paper clips in little cups according to size and color seldom leave pamphlets lying around, much less where a good twirl of the casters could crease them irrevocably.

I retrieved the straggler. I expected it was just another magazine from the banquet. I knew how wild these folks who hand out playbills can get. Magazines everywhere. No chair safe.

It wasn't a magazine. It was a brochure from an auction, turned open to a page depicting an old violin. From the number of commas and zeros hovering around the estimated bid price it was evidently a very expensive old violin.

I checked the date at the bottom. June 2008. For some reason Victoria—or someone sitting in Victoria's chair—had been reminiscing over an auction which had taken place over five years ago. I identified two possibilities for this: A) She—or someone sitting in her chair—had been involved in the purchase of this violin. B) Someone sitting here—maybe she—had taken part in the sale of it.

The rest of my detailed analysis would have to wait. The sound of a door slamming across the hall caused me to spring forward, scattering paper clips everywhere.

I attempted to reassemble them from memory—silver before gold, gold next to copper—then squished them altogether, hurried out of the office, and scooted down the hall.

By my count, that made three furtive exits from the vestibule in just under an hour. Five if you counted Victoria's and Fleet's. (I hadn't seen them go, but let's assume theirs were at least semi-furtive.) Something about that place seemed to promote rapid egresses.

I stumbled on Fleet in the Pendleton Library. He looked no more furtive than usual, not even semi-furtive. He was sitting at one of the tables which had not yet been folded up and put away. Hutton, Ate and Lesley were also there, listening as he related some useful tidbit.

He signaled to me as I arrived. "Ah, Johnny, there you are. I was just bringing Hutton and the ladies up to speed."

I could stand some speed upbringing myself. I took a seat next to Lesley, who leaned in and told me not to worry, she was able to reserve the hall for our wedding reception, no problem. They gave us an excellent price. Our credit cards had no limits, right?

I was in no mood to discuss the epic debt my fiancée had secured on our behalf tonight. No doubt the expenditure would go down in song and story, and I could learn the totals then.

"What did Victoria Walters have to say?" I asked Fleet.

"Not too much. She was starting to tell me something about Chester Callas when Lyle strolled in and interrupted."

I snorted. He would stroll in at that moment. "I tell you that man wants watching."

"Yes…Well, anyway, his presence curbed her remarks. I'm going to meet with her tomorrow. Maybe we can get the whole scoop then."

I looked to Hutton, then to the girls, then from the girls back to Fleet.

Someone had to say it; it might as well be me. "Anyone else notice her eyes?"

Lesley, whose own eyes were pretty foxy, said they were lovely, weren't they? You don't come across many black women with eyes that shade, do you? Hutton agreed that Victoria's eyes were nice, and most unusual, although he had seen black people with blue eyes before. Of course, some of them could have been wearing contact lenses. This prompted Ate to ask if this discussion wasn't racist in some way. Seemed racist to her. Lesley saw her point. Perhaps it was a smidgeon racist. What did Hutton think?

Fleet weighed in with the tiebreaker. "I don't think Johnny intended to discuss the allure of Victoria's eyes, attractive though they are. I believe he was alluding to the moniker *Ol' Blue Eyes*."

I thanked him. "What if Victoria was Chester's version of Ol' Blue Eyes?"

Hutton didn't think her that old, really, although it was difficult to tell with women of color sometimes. Lesley agreed that many African American women hid their age very well, didn't they, and Ate chimed in to say that this conversation definitely felt racist to her. Or, if not racist, at least it had a racial undertone. What did her dad think?

I could see we had gone off topic again.

"The clue, people! Chester's last words were 'Frank Sinatra.' I find that significant."

Hutton thought it somewhat significant. He wasn't certain I knew this, but Frank Sinatra was also known as Ol' Blue Eyes.

"I know he was!" I roared. I lowered my voice. The librarian might be lurking. "That's what I've been saying. Perhaps Chester's last words were his whimsical way of indicating Victoria Walters."

Hutton agreed that Chester never was much for keeping track of people's names. "Maybe there is something to this blue-eyed concept."

"Yes, but lots of people have blue eyes," Lesley argued.

"But not that many African American people do," Hutton pointed out. "And Chester was a Brit. A blue-eyed black person might have struck him as more unusual."

"You know what I think," said Ate, and I waved my hand impatiently to indicate that I knew and didn't care. What difference did it make if Chet's clue was racist? He was dead.

"The point is, could that have been his intention? Could he have been fingering Victoria Walters as his killer?"

"It's possible," answered Fleet. "It fits with the Sinatra theme. Speaking of which, I shared your observation about Lyle Pendleton with everyone. The Chairman angle."

I said ah. And what was everyone's reaction to my Lyle Pendleton observation?

Hutton thought it had promise. As we may or may not have heard, Frank Sinatra was frequently called the Chairman of the Board himself. Ate thought it sounded a bit thin to her, and Lesley wondered how many nicknames Sinatra had. No one found the discussion racist.

I saw Fleet glance at his watch. Were we keeping him from something? "I believe everything hinges on one small…"

What everything hinged on, and how small it was, we would have to wait to hear. Nathaniel Goody had joined our little party, along with Tanya Saxon.

The late hour didn't seem to affect her. She might be as old as time itself, but that didn't mean she had to give into it. It could have been one in the afternoon for the vim with which she approached our table. I wanted to hate her, but I didn't have the energy.

"I thought you'd all like to know," trilled Nate Goody, "that I've found it. It was exactly where I left it."

Fleet smiled. "The Enescu score?"

"No, no. The bottle of tuica. The rhapsody hasn't turned up," he said. "But it shall—it shall. I just need to remember. It only requires a bit of brainpower."

I sagged in my chair. I felt encouraged until he mentioned brainpower. Brainpower was not Nate's strong suit.

Fleet didn't sag, but when he leaned back it was atop a fairly unenthused elbow, an elbow that had expected better things. "Delighted you found your case of booze, Nate—"

"Not the case," corrected the dean, "just a bottle. The search goes on for the case."

"Yes, and one wishes you Godspeed with that. However, I am much more interested in the whereabouts of the Enescu score. Even though yours is only a copy, I would like to examine it."

Tanya Saxon had a thought. "If viewing the score is so important to you, Mr. Fleet, perhaps Lyle Pendleton has a copy."

Nate blinked at her.

"He was privy to the discussions with Mr. Callas, was he not?"

Nate said he supposed he was. It was a thought. "He's probably gone to bed now, though."

"Tomorrow then," said Tanya. "Till then," she nodded and glided from our presence.

Nate followed, not so much gliding as clumping, and Fleet resumed his seat. I had intended to stand when the old gal left us, but I was too tired. I cast her a sort of standing nod as she went, and that would just have to do.

"I suppose we should call it an evening ourselves," Fleet decided.

No one argued, least of all me. I couldn't wait to crawl in between the sheets at our hotel. It was quite a drive from here but well worth it. They had nice sheets.

Fleet corrected me on a point. "Not the hotel, Johnny, the dorms. It's summer, and because of this many of the rooms are vacant. Lyle Pendleton has generously offered us the use of a couple of them."

I really must have been tired. It sounded like he had said *Not the hotel, Johnny, the dorms...Lyle has generously offered us the use of a couple of them...*

Fleet assured me that he had said that very thing.

"I called and had the hotel send over our bags. We're staying in Adagio Hall. As you know, it's quite a drive back to the hotel—"

I didn't think it was *that* long a drive, really—

"—and it's better if we can be on hand to pick up the threads on the case first thing tomorrow. You want to pick up threads, don't you, Johnny? Of course you do! Besides, we wouldn't want to scorn Lyle's generous offer, now would we? Of course we wouldn't. Right then, off we go, people."

Off we went, my own person not so chipperly. Just what I most desired—to be back in school again.

I used to have bad dreams about this.

I'd find myself wandering around a campus much like this one, not knowing who I was or what I was doing, and then I'd suddenly realize I'd forgotten to attend half my required lectures that semester (when, in reality, I never missed more than eight or nine when I was in school).

Of course, in the dream, I wasn't dressed in a tux. Usually I was in my underwear. Once I had on a Scottish kilt; I don't know why.

As if sleeping in dorms wasn't awesome enough, there weren't any cabs available at that time of night. Fleet suggested we take advantage of the pleasant evening and walk to Adagio Hall: a charming uphill hike in dress pants and loafers.

I would have preferred the kilt.

The ladies had it tougher, I suppose. They had on heels. Eventually these snapped off, though, so I don't know what they were grousing about. While we walked—limped, crawled—I asked Fleet why he thought the missing score was so important. It was only a printout.

"There are plenty of collectors who would pay a small fortune for it, not just the manuscript but the discovery: a previously unheard piece of music. Some might even kill for it. If Nate's copy has gone missing, and Chester's original has yet to be accounted for, we might be looking at a very meticulous thief, systematically eliminating the competition as he prepares the market for his plunder."

I nodded, the gesture causing me to fall behind a few steps. He walked so damn fast. "Would Romania kill for it?" I asked, hurrying to catch up. I had experience with governments clinging pretty tightly to their national treasures.

Fleet wasn't certain about kill. Romania, as a whole, didn't roll like that. But there could be some Romanian somewhere prepared to kill to bring home this prize. Why did I ask?

"I saw a man tonight."

Fleet found this fascinating. He had seen several men. Women too.

"Possibly a Romanian," I added, thanking him to knock off the sarcasm—I had blisters. "He had a sort of Eastern European look to him, very Romanian-ish."

"Not exactly extraordinary at a dinner honoring Romania's most famous composer. Where did you see this man?"

I explained about running into my uncle—telling Fleet not to get his hopes up, the congressman probably didn't do it. I mentioned the man at the top of the stairs and Victoria's open office door, touching lightly on my explorations within.

I had piqued his interest. "And it seemed to you that the lock had been forced?"

I didn't know about forced, but it had been ridden pretty hard and put away wet.

He paused on the path, mostly to allow the rest of our team to catch up. "This is interesting, Johnny. After I left Lyle and Victoria, she must have been joined by Sergei Brodovitch, the pianist. I saw the pair of them talking on one of the library balconies shortly before you came in. That would have given your mysterious Romanian ample time to search Victoria's office."

"Who's Sergei Brodovitch?"

"A pianist," said Fleet, looking at his watch again.

I had gathered that much. "Is he an instructor?"

"More of a student professor. He's a phenom, you know."

"One of these ex-child prodigies?"

"It would seem so, although no one around here ever saw him perform as a child. He simply showed up one day as a young man and wowed the board with his magic fingers. They gave him a full scholarship. He's Czech."

With a name like Brodovitch I didn't think he was from Albuquerque.

"He gives advanced instruction to some of the more promising students and occasionally accompanies the Pendleton Orchestra in their Sunday performances. He was at the dinner tonight and has an office adjacent the library, along with Nate Goody, Victoria Walters, Lyle Pendleton and Tanya Saxon."

I said ah again. Another suspect. Perhaps it was his door I had heard slamming while I skulked inside Victoria's office. I tried to recall if it had been a phenomenal slam, the kind of slam that would have preceded from the magic fingers of a genius, or just the regular kind. I couldn't remember.

"Leaving Czechs aside for the moment," I went on, "you believe my Romanian, if he was Romanian, could have some bearing on the case?"

Fleet said possibly, quite possibly, and we continued our trek.

We eventually punched in at our destination at 3 a.m., finding our accommodations exactly how I pictured them: small and sparse, like an oversized pup tent. Not that oversized. They had bunk beds, actual freaking bunk beds.

Our luggage was scattered hither and yon, but nobody seemed that interested in luggage. The girls flopped down on the bunks across the hall. They didn't even bother to slip out of their gowns first. They just lay there, stacked side by side like designer cordwood, while Hutton and I took a couple of chairs in the other room and put our feet up.

Fleet attended to more pressing matters. An undergraduate had materialized in the doorway, explaining how our luggage had been delivered from the hotel. He indicated the luggage. There was something else, he said, and I saw him tug at a long leather strap leading offstage. The way he struggled with it reminded me of a tentative fisherman reeling in what he suspects might be an unexploded depth charge. An instant later, a small, scruffy Maltese danced in, nearly choking herself on her leash.

Fleet smiled. The dog Pixie was here, the legacy of his beloved late wife. Now I knew why he had been checking his watch all evening. Maltese hate to be kept waiting.

After being cooped up in a hotel shuttle for an hour, the cramped dorm must have seemed palatial to her. She darted off. There was nothing her snuffling nose couldn't reach, and she wanted to take it all in and absorb every inch in one doggy instant.

Having bounded up on the lower bunk, then off, then up, she squealed over to the bathroom, sent something crashing in the offing, and then galloped out to my side, where she proceeded to put her paws up on my dress pants and stare longingly into my eyes. I had seen that look before.

The undergraduate appeared well out of it. Fleet tipped him—handsomely, I should hope—and off he went, sucking the leash burn on his hand.

He returned a few seconds later, using his other hand to slip Fleet a sheet of paper one of his police buddies had left for him.

Fleet glanced at the sheet and nodded, but most of his attention was concentrated on his dog and her deep, wistful look.

We both knew what she wanted.

Sadly—and it pains me to say this—his pup had developed a drinking problem. I don't know if she picked it up from her pals or saw it on TV, but our fine furry friend had what is known as a bottled-water fetish. No other beverage would do.

You had to serve it by hand, in a glass, preferably chilled and always with the correct tilt, or she would get it up her nose. Fiji was her brand of choice.

At the moment, I was the man with the liquid. I had secured a bottle from the dorm vending machine on our way in, and had barely put away half before the little wombat came knocking on my knee, demanding her cut.

I heaved a sigh. I had tried resistance in the past, never to any avail, but in recent weeks I had basically resigned myself to the role of canine sommelier. I poured out a splash in a mug and watched with no love-light in my eyes as she slurped.

"What's on the paper?" I asked, after Pixie had smacked her lips and tottered away.

"Phone extensions," answered Fleet. "I had a friend pull the list for us. If I'm right, some internal extension called Chester Callas on that library line just before he fell to his death. These are the likely candidates."

Nathaniel Goody, ext. 21336
Lyle Pendleton, ext. 23285
Tanya Saxon, ext. 26986
Victoria Walters, ext. 27156
Henry Pratt, ext. 31332
Sergei Brodovitch, ext. 31385

"Who's Henry Pratt?" I asked.

Fleet wasn't sure. Another of the student instructors, he thought, but he hadn't met him. We had that treat in store for later on.

I handed the sheet to Hutton, who had a question of his own. "If one of these people phoned Chester just before he went over the rail, then it stands to reason that they couldn't also be the killer. No one can be in two places at once."

Fleet never liked the word *couldn't* and thought even less of the phrase *no one*. He agreed that the logistics posed certain obstacles. "We'll have to mull on it."

And with that mull in mind, he scooped Pixie up and left us with one final thought for the evening:

"It's possible the caller's role was merely to keep Chester Callas occupied, distract him. Or the person may have had nothing to do with the murder at all. Either way, the caller has information, information on Chester's last moments. I believe it is on this information, no matter how small, that the murder hinges."

I nodded, contentedly this time. So this was the hinge he had started to describe to us in the library.

I was glad he finally told us. I wouldn't have been able to get to sleep if he hadn't.

10 — Curious Movements

Actually, I wouldn't have offered stellar odds on my getting to sleep regardless.

Those bunk beds for one; the stuffy confines for another. There was hardly enough air in the place to keep a soda bubble afloat.

And that wasn't all. Just to put the icing on the adagio, I wouldn't be staying with Lesley. Somehow I had drawn Hutton as bunkmate.

I'm not certain how it happened. One minute I was crawling into my teeny-weeny bed, expecting my fiancée to snuggle in beside me; the next, my fiancée had taken residence across the hall, in a teeny-weeny bed of her own.

She was keeping Ate company, she explained. It seemed Ate didn't feel comfortable sharing a room with Hutton at this point in their relationship. They were taking things slow, Ate and Hutton were. Very, very slow.

So, with only the two rooms between us, unless one of us wanted to crowd in with Enescu Fleet and the Maltese, the girls were taking one, and the boys another. It was phenomenal how well the math worked out there.

I tried to reason with the ladies. I reminded them that both rooms had bunk beds—ample, wondrous bunk beds—so there was really nothing preventing the virtuous female, Ate for example, from enjoying a chaste evening alone with a virtuous male. Hutton, in this case.

My arguments failed to move them. It was like trying to reason with Pixie on one of her thirsty afternoons. Ate pointed out that even if she and Hutton didn't share a bed, she hadn't packed a nightshirt or pajamas. She liked to sleep *au naturel.* Now how would that be?

If I had any rejoinder to this it withered away, probably somewhere around the phrase *au naturel.*

Ten minutes later, after Hutton had washed and brushed and made all sorts of racket in the bath, he bounded into the bunk above me, and there we lay, he shifting and creaking to get situated, I wishing I had some variety of scimitar to jab through the mattress. Eventually he got still, and I was at liberty to lie back and glare out into the moonlight.

You had to love how things were shaping up. I had no woman; no sense of what I was doing; and, thanks to Pixie, my bed linen now smelled like a Malta dog kennel. It was just like college the first time.

"Sorry about this, Hath," spoke up my roommate, and I had to poke my head out into the aisle to see if I had heard right.

Hutton apologizing? It was almost as rare as Uncle George asking for my help.

"I guess I wasn't up to trying my hand at seduction tonight."

This was a relief, I assured him.

"I know you would have preferred Lesley in here—"

"Yes."

"But if you want my honest opinion, I'm not sure you could have gotten up to much. It would be like trying to entwine bodies inside a pea pod, these beds."

I didn't want his honest opinion, and I would have gladly given entwining a try. Personally, I had always found pea pods the most erotic of all the vegetable pods.

But, again, it wasn't a huge deal. "I'm good," I said, frowning. There was something I still didn't understand. "On the subject of entwining, I thought you and Ate—"

"No," he replied.

There was a slight strain in his voice. That could have been the bunk beds, however.

"We were heading along the proper path for a while there," he elaborated, "but then she took that trip to Spain with her father last spring, and it threw off our schedule. You can't bung a two month hiatus in the middle of burgeoning romance and expect it to keep on burgeoning. The bud goes stale. I wouldn't put it past the old man to have planned it that way," he sniffed, and I could detect dudgeon in that sniff.

I wouldn't put it past him either. Fathers are like that, even hot-blooded rogues like Enescu Fleet.

"By the time she returned home, it was like we had been sent back to *Go* and not collected our two hundred guineas. Then she started focusing on that hospitality business of hers, and I was struggling to find cases, and well, we can't seem to get on track now."

"Right," I said. I was sorry I brought it up.

"The thing is, we got off on the wrong foot right off the bat," he continued. "We started seeing each other around the holidays. Not smart. It's never easy getting something hot and heavy going in November. It's not a holiday conducive to sex, your Thanksgiving."

I supposed it wasn't.

"I'm not certain why you have it, honestly. I mean, if there was anything I'd want to be thankful for, it wouldn't be some giant roasted buzzard. It would be—well, that's neither here nor there."

I could see Hutton's off-again, off-again romance with the Fleet daughter was not a pleasant topic for the wee hours. I switched to something a little less emotionally charged. "So how about this Callas?" I remarked.

"What about him?" Hutton asked.

I didn't know what about him. Just sort of, well, him. "His murder and all."

"Yes."

I sensed an implied sniff there. His yes had a *good-riddance* flavor to it.

I soldiered on. "I still don't quite remember him. He was at school with us?"

Hutton didn't reply. He seemed to be brooding. After a span of silence, fairly sniffy, he replied, "He wasn't there long. About halfway through our first year his folks took him out and placed him at some fancy academy for the arts to study music. Kind of like this place but for the younger kiddles."

I said oh. "You seem to remember a lot about him."

"I knew him before then. When we were young."

Now we were getting somewhere. I knew next to nothing of Hutton's early childhood. In fact, it didn't seem like he had much of a childhood at all before we met. Had you asked me, I would have thought he had hatched from a pod or something—a pea pod perhaps.

"Was he as loathsome as a kid as he would become later?"

"Pretty much, if not loathsomer."

I found this hard to fathom. "More loathsome?"

"The loathsomest," said Hutton.

As I say, I'm pretty good at picking up on subtle nuances in people's speech. I thought I spotted a slab of subtlety here. "You didn't like him much, did you?"

"I hated him."

"Why?" I asked. "I mean, besides the obvious reasons."

"Why does anyone hate anyone?" wondered Hutton.

It was much too late in the day to start delving into these philosophical matters now. "He must have done something to you?" I prompted.

"Such as what?"

I had no idea. "Swiped your favorite blankie during nap time? Gobbled down the last snickerdoodle out of your lunch pail? How should I know?" I said.

I heard the bed creak in contemplation. Or maybe that was just the struggle of a tall man doing battle with a miniature mattress.

"He and I were in a sort of junior honor program at the local nursery. Despite his flaws, Chester had an amazing brain. He had this amazing capacity for remembering everything he saw, even as a child. He never forgot anything—I think it was one of the things that distorted his personality. We were considered two of the more gifted children in the neighborhood, so naturally our parents pitted us against each other from time to time."

I said naturally, naturally. We were making real progress here, I felt. "You were considered gifted?" I clarified.

"It was never anything he actually *did* to you," mused Hutton, ignoring my question and continuing to unburden himself. "He didn't *do* anything to anyone, really. He just had a way of keeping people under his thumb. Even as a child."

I knew the type. Congressman Hathaway had always been that way. Until tonight, that is. "Kept people under his thumb how?"

"If you don't mind," said Hutton, creaking again, "I'd rather not talk about Chester Callas anymore."

But I did mind. I minded a ton. Our time was not up here. "Yes, but—"

"Drop it, Hath."

Fine, I told him. And there *was* dudgeon in my reply. I didn't want to talk about his stupid childhood anyway.

We passed a moody silence amongst the collegiate doll furniture. "Apropos of nothing," I remarked, "have you ever noticed how much my uncle George looks like an elderly Frank Sinatra?"

"Night, Hath," said Hutton, and for the first time in a long time, I found myself in complete agreement with the man.

I slept.

But not for long. Not in Adagio Hall. It was a wonder to me that the young musicians who stayed here didn't nod off in the middle of their scales every morning.

I did sleep a little bit, though, and while I slept, I dreamt I was in Vegas, opening for a duet of Nate Goody and Tanya Saxon—Lyle Pendleton on bass. Ate was working the audience as an old-timey cigar and cigarette girl, only she was nude.

(If anyone would like to turn that into something sexual, I'd be very interested to know how.)

Nude Ate was on her way up to the stage to light my stogie (in the dream), when I was awoken by a curious presence in the room. Normally, having Hutton asleep above me would have been curious enough, but this presence was curiouser. It was on the move.

For a second, I thought Pixie might have returned with a view to rubbing her paws on some patch of sheet she had previously overlooked. But it wasn't Pixie. The figure traversing the length of the room was considerably larger and humanoid, wearing a hat. I could see the brim in silhouette.

I shot a hand out toward the night table and, after sending my phone, my wallet and my half bottle of water flying, connected with the light.

The presence revealed itself to be a man of about twenty: round, stubbly cheeks; large, darting eyes; a barrel-chested physique; and a cool-jazz chic to his clothing. His blazer was dark and flung over his shoulder, his tie thin and open at the collar.

The hat was a trilby, a slim-billed variety popular among modern hipsters and the occasional Fifties ad man. I used to have one just like it, though I never considered myself hip (or likely to come up with a decent jingle for Alka-Seltzer).

"What the hell?" I asked this apparition, and the man raised a meaty eyebrow.

"Easy does it, guy. Don't blow a gasket."

From somewhere above, Hutton grumbled, "Five more minutes."

I scowled. If this was his method for dealing with retro-style assassins, I could see why he and Ate were having trouble. Girls liked go-getters. So did I.

"Who the hell are you?" I asked the assassin.

"Name's Henry Pratt." He gave me the once-over. "You're kinda old to be a student," he said, the stubble contorting into a grin. "You must be with the shamus."

Maybe we were; maybe we weren't. It all depended on what a shamus was exactly. "How do you mean old?" I asked.

Henry Pratt said, "Well, like old, man, *old*," and I nodded. I saw what he meant.

Henry Pratt? Henry Pratt? Where had we heard of a Henry Pratt recently? Then I had it. Our AWOL phone extension. The suspect we had yet to meet. "You work here?"

Pratt said you know it, sport, and I nodded again. I liked *man* better than *sport*, I think. Just a personal preference.

"And sorry about startling you, champ,"—*champ* wasn't bad. "Sometimes I use these rooms to flop in after a session. Nobody seems to mind, and usually the building's half empty during summer. You dig?"

I dug. As long as he kept his flopping away from the girls' room—the Pendleton's answer to a French nudist colony—I dug him the most. "Session?"

"Band practice. I help run the band program here at the school. I'm also a student, see, but the band, that's my line. I'm drums."

This surprised me. "The Pendleton Institute of Music has a school band?"

"You know it. The best band."

"But why a band?" I asked. "I mean, isn't that like the Red Sox having an office softball team?"

Pratt didn't care much for my analogy. "Band music is music just like any other, man. You need to study it, embrace it. Look at all the bandleaders at schools and universities. How do you think those cats train?"

I never really thought about it. I just figured they threw something together.

"Were you at the banquet tonight?"

"No, you mook. I told you; we had practice. The band program runs all year round, and you gotta practice if you want to be tight for your gigs."

If he said so. From the band music I had always heard, it didn't seem to make much of a difference either way.

He threw his jacket on a chair and flipped his hat onto a peg across the room. "So what's your label, daddy-o?"

I told him my label was John Hathaway. *Johnny* I reserve for people who don't wake me at four thirty in the morning. I got out of bed and shook hands.

"Who's that?" Hutton asked, rolling over and blinking into the light. If I didn't know better, I'd have said there was a hint of the ham in the way he spoke that line. I wondered if he had been awake all along.

"Henry Pratt," I said.

Hutton said no kidding. Extension 31332 in person. Donning the eyewear, he jumped down from the bunk and pressed the flesh.

Fortunately for me and Henry, Hutton did not sleep *au naturel.*

"Hutton," repeated the music man. "Is that Hutton *Something* or *Something* Hutton?"

"Actually, it's an interesting story," said Hutton Neither, and Pratt asked him to spill it. He liked interesting stories.

Left to his own devices, I knew Hutton would have turned the anecdote into one of those epics Plutarch used to regale the Romans with. Jumping in ahead of him, I remarked that it was just a little play on words having to do with the first and last initials of his name.

"Oh yeah? And what first and last initials are those?" asked Pratt.

"E. F.," I said. "Short for Enescu Fleet."

"No kidding. Isn't that the old-timer's handle?"

It was. It was also Hutton's handle. "Back in English boarding school, he never really cared for it. He insisted everyone call him E. F., never revealing his full name. I've often wondered how he squared the administration on that. The teachers complied, and eventually his classmates followed. But with time weighing heavy on our hands, and amusements few and far between, we had to find something to bring a smile to our young faces. E. F. became E. F. Hutton and sometime after that, just Hutton. These diversions kept us off the streets."

"No fooling. You a shamus too?" Pratt asked him.

Hutton agreed he was. Although he preferred the term gumshoe.

"And you're some kind of nephew or grandson?"

I took up the slack again. He and Fleet weren't technically related, no. Hutton was the adopted son of Fleet's third cousin. Anything less and his wooing of Fleet's daughter would have given one and all the heebie-jeebies. (It already did with Fleet.)

My explanation seemed to satisfy Pratt for now. "I should be going," he announced. "Let you cats get some sleep. Mind if I take a swig of your H2O?" he asked.

He could have all the swigs he wanted, I told him. As long as he didn't expect me to hold the drink out for him in a tiny glass.

"Say that again, bud?"

"Never mind."

He left soon after, humming an invigorating tune, and Hutton sat down on my pillow. Hutton, Maltese—it was all good.

He was looking pensive again. "Did that guy remind you of anyone?"

I stared at the closed door. "Bluto?"

"I was actually thinking of someone else."

"Young Bluto?"

"Frank Sinatra."

I didn't see it. Sinatra was never that strapping, especially in his youth. Pratt was too beefy.

"I'm not talking about how he looked. I'm talking about how he acted. His speech. There was a lounge-singer quality to it."

I shrugged. "You think all Americans have a lounge-singer quality to their speech. Besides, Henry Pratt couldn't be the man Chet meant to finger. He wasn't even at the dinner."

"So he says."

I shook my head. "I think you're off this time. Yes, his diction was a touch affected, but you know these band guys: they're odd."

"Maybe you're right. So you didn't find him the slightest bit Sinatra in demeanor?"

"Not especially. Now my uncle George on the other hand—"

Hutton grunted yes, my uncle George, and climbed back into his bunk, using my pillow as a footstool.

I followed his excellent example, flopping onto the snarled sheets I had come to know and love. I hit the light switch.

"Night, daddy-o," I muttered.

"Night, you mook," he replied.

11 — Rest

When I finally slept, I dreamt of Vegas again, only this time Henry Pratt was headlining, Victoria Walters was conducting a brass band, and Ate wasn't selling cigars. She was, however, still nude.

At one point somebody must have played off-key, because Victoria began slashing through the band with a meat cleaver. Henry responded by withdrawing a battle-ax from one of the tubas, and the sound of all the hot blades on cold instruments shook me awake with a shudder.

I shot up, smacking my head solidly on the top bunk.

I could still hear the clamor. It wasn't hot blades, however. Someone in a nearby room was tuning a trumpet. Or murdering a goose, I couldn't tell which. The trumpet soon took a backseat to a couple violins. Then an oboe came online, several clarinets, a handful of drums, and what sounded like a zither. Apparently there were plenty of students at Pendleton who liked flopping in Adagio Hall in the summer months.

I climbed out of bed. Seeing Hutton wasn't in his, I went looking for him (and/or a meat cleaver).

I didn't have much luck with the cutlery, but I did find Hutton in the kitchen with Fleet and Pixie. The canine was lapping from a cup, held out by Hutton (sound asleep). Both master and Maltese appeared well rested, Fleet in his quintessential tweed blazer and vest, mutt in basic white fur. Hutton, snoozing quietly in his T-shirt and PJs, looked like something the pup had dug up from the backyard. I could only assume I looked pretty much the same, with the addition of the bump where the bunk had crescendoed off my temple.

I crowded into the tiny kitchen and grunted good morning. I say kitchen, but it was more of a kitchenette. Call it a reduced-fat kitchenette. Four by six feet, if that.

Fleet shifted aside to make room, and I saw they were examining the contents of an antique travel chest. Chester's chest. It took up the entire surface of the Formica table.

"The police retrieved this from Chester's hotel room this morning," answered Fleet, in reply to my silent query. "I had a friend on the force bring it by on its way to the station."

I nodded. Always nice to give one's personal effects a break while on tour.

"The messenger is waiting in the hall, so we can't keep him long."

I yawned. A fellow courier. When not assisting one of the Fleets in their investigations, I'd been known to shuttle the occasional package or two. I did it freelance. I hoped my counterpart in the hall was enjoying the *Squawk Symphony in B Sharp Squawk*. I suspected he wasn't.

I asked where the girls were. "Making pancakes next door" would have been my preferred answer, but it wasn't my day for having my preferences met. They were sleeping in. I would have liked to have known how, but women always have been a mystery to me.

"Why didn't the cops bring this junk to your room?"

Fleet explained that his room wasn't available for junk viewing at the moment. It was being brightened up by the housekeeper.

"Housekeeper?" I repeated. The dorms had housekeeping?

He shook his well-groomed noggin. "I didn't stay in the dorms last night, Johnny. I stayed with Lyle Pendleton at his villa."

I drew myself up, rapping the back of my ungroomed noggin on the doorframe.

"You stayed at a villa! Lyle Pendleton's villa! Lyle Pendleton has a villa?" I asked.

"On the other side of the campus. I figured you wouldn't be interested. He only had the single accommodation. One guest room, queen-sized bed, not much of a view."

I would have thundered something about his queen beds and inadequate views, but didn't feel the ancient acoustics could contain my outburst. No sense in bringing down chunks of drywall and practicing clarinetists from above.

"I need a drink," I said instead.

Fleet pointed to some fresh coffee and orange juice on the counter. I was thinking more along the lines of bourbon with a splash of rye, but the OJ would do for now.

Reaching for the pitcher, I tripped over a tiny coffin someone had left strewn across the kitchen tile. The thunder in my sternum made another passing rumble, but I kept it under wraps, mostly because I was curious about this miniature sarcophagus.

It turned out to be a violin case. Chester's case. With a sullen glare, I propped it up on Hutton's lap and took a shot of orange backed with a coffee chaser.

"Do you notice anything unusual about these items?" Fleet asked me.

I looked them over. A few too many combs and hair products. More black silk than I would ever wear. But basically a pretty typical assortment for the traveling Englishman.

"Nothing seems out of place?" he said.

I looked again. "The rhapsody isn't here."

Fleet smiled indulgently. "No, but that's not necessarily significant. Chester wouldn't have needed it for his performance—Hutton tells me he would have long since memorized both the transcription and the original score—and he wouldn't have risked leaving the latter in his hotel room. It would have been locked away somewhere for safekeeping."

"Though hopefully not with Nate Goody," I suggested. "On the subject of the score, did you find out whether Lyle Pendleton had a copy?"

"Not yet. We haven't had a chance to speak. Evidently something got him out of bed bright and early this morning."

I nodded. Maybe someone had been strangling a tuba in the room down the hall from him.

I peered down at the luggage again. If it wasn't the score…

"No curling iron?" I hazarded.

Fleet gave his head another soft waggle. "You're looking at it the wrong way. Don't look for what is missing; identify what is here and shouldn't be."

And so saying, he dipped his brow toward the sarcophagus. I stared. Chester's violin? "But he did play the violin," I said. "Learned it as a kiddle, Hutton informs me."

"Yes, and he was to play it for us last night. So what was it doing in his hotel room?"

He had a point. What was it?

"Even the most accomplished virtuoso," said Fleet, "would have a hard time performing a transcription of Enescu's third Romanian Rhapsody with his violin across town."

His words began to pierce the fog. "It should have been with him at the banquet?"

"Exactly."

But it wasn't. It was in his room. What was this Callas playing at? Not the violin, clearly. "Do you think he had two?"

"No."

"Then I'm stymied."

Fleet was too, as I suspect Hutton would have been, had he been conscious. Glancing across the table, the elder PI shook the younger, causing Hutton to spring up in his chair.

"Yes, Countess," he uttered, "but the jewels are no longer in your bodice, are they…?"

He paused, blinking at us. "What?"

I'll hand it to Hutton: he did have a nice instant-awake feature. "So what's the score?" he asked, sipping from his juice.

"No score," I replied. "Violin."

He gazed down at it. He didn't appear the slightest bit curious how the instrument had materialized in his lap. "This was among Chester's hotel effects? He should have had it with him at the banquet."

A good point, agreed Fleet. A very good point.

We left the girls to their rest. If they could sleep through the Adagio warm-ups, then more power to them.

After Hutton and I had brightened ourselves up, the detectives and I headed out to see Victoria Walters. It was roughly eight a.m.

The stroll across the campus went down much better in the daylight hours. It was warm but not too warm, the sun was shining but not too shiny, another August breeze was blowing, and I had on comfortable shoes: everything a man needs to greet the morning. Add to that a good pair of jeans and a lightweight golf shirt, and I could take in the rolling hills and shady oaks with a contented smile. Last night, I had viewed every foot of the winding path as one more sullen step to go before we slept, but today I actually welcomed the exercise. It was nice.

I never cared much for school when I was in it, but I could almost see the fascination today. I wasn't about to toddle off to the registrar's or anything—just as well, I doubted they'd be clamoring for my limited skills on the harmonica—but for the first time since we got there, I was enjoying my visit.

The lack of scholars helped. We spotted a few young musicians as we walked, a handful rushing to some summer class, and one asleep under a shady oak, but that was about it. This sparsity only added to the soothing effect. Nothing disrupts a picturesque college campus more than a bunch of students.

As we strolled, I filled in Fleet on Henry Pratt's visit. He didn't seem very interested in Hutton's Rat Pack correlation, but that didn't deter me. I'd known Fleet to take things on board, not mention them for days, and then, having added a slight twist of his own, reveal them again at some precise dramatic moment, to the amazement of all involved.

He agreed that we should probably check Pratt's alibi, as well as his association with the other members of the Pendleton administration. The suspects, as I liked to call them.

I was still a little hazy on how the murder went down. The call. The shove. The knife. In a way, it all fit; in another, it didn't fit at all. It was not unusual for me to have no clue who had done it, but this was the first time I had no clue *how* they could have done it.

We reached the back entrance to the library but made it no farther than the sliding doors. There was an officer there, not one of our chums, and he informed us that the building was still a crime scene and only certain persons were allowed access while the detectives finished up. Apparently this guest list did not include tiny Maltese dogs with manic looks in their eyes.

Fleet had faced this kind of discrimination before. I'd seen him get the pup into some pretty exclusive digs in his time, but this evidently was not one of those times. The officer was adamant.

Fortunately Hutton offered to shoulder the dog owner's burden. He didn't mind the fresh air, and if nature's splendor began to wear on him, he could always head up the path to Lyle's villa.

It was decided, then. Hutton and Pixie would continue their walkies; the cop would go on standing guard, content in the knowledge that he had kept his murder scene free of Maltese piddle; and Fleet and I would keep our appointment with Victoria. Everyone was happy.

Given a choice, I probably would have preferred to question Lyle: corner him on some secluded veranda of his villa, order a refreshing iced tea and scone from his housekeeper, and demand he disgorge his copy of the Enescu score. But Victoria was good too.

Might as well see what Ol' Blue Eyes had to say for herself.

12 — Old Scores

Unlike Pixie, I made it inside without any objections. (Slurp on that, furball.)

Even Victoria Walters didn't seem to mind I was there. She didn't seem to notice me one way or another, in fact, which is almost as good. Either way you sliced it, I was that much more ahead of the game compared with my previous visit to her office. No more sneaking through doorways and poking around dimly lit corners for me.

As before, the newly appointed orchestra director looked determined to disclose something. The night's rest had only accentuated this resolve. Once we had all grabbed a seat, Fleet across from her desk, I a little off to the side (in a dimly lit corner), she commenced:

"There's something I need to tell you about Chester Callas, Ef, something I didn't tell the police. It's bound to come out in your investigations, and you might as well hear it from me."

"I'm here to help, Vee," he replied. (Apparently they were on *Ef* and *Vee* terms now.)

A frown had creased her heart-shaped face. I hadn't noticed before how much the turn of her lips could affect her entire appearance. I guess when you're busy spilling brandy on a woman's dress you tend to miss these things.

"I actually met Callas years ago," she began. "You might say we had a past."

I glanced up. I wouldn't have pegged Chet and her as a couple, and felt she could have done better.

"When I was still performing, he reviewed my *Well-Tempered Clavier.*"

I expected something kinkier than this. I wasn't entirely sure what a clavier was, but as long as it remained well-tempered…

"This was five years ago. I had put together some fugue variations, arranged for cello and violin, and Callas represented a record label looking to produce us. They used to send him out to concerts to scout new talent."

She paused, staring off into the invisible past. "I knew what a bastard he could be, even before we'd met. He had torpedoed so many young musicians, many close to his own age. Just brutalized them. And I wasn't that young anymore. I couldn't afford to keep living from performance to performance. I needed a windfall, and a label deal could provide it."

She hesitated again. "It was a stupid thing to do—I know that now—but after the concert I met with him at his office. I begged him to give us the green light. Begged—" She smiled mirthlessly. "I only wish I had begged. I tried to bribe him."

Fleet pondered this revelation. "And what did he say to that?"

"He laughed in my face. Who knew he had standards, right? It was only after I'd left that I learned he had already green-lighted us. Well, two of us anyway—he savaged the second violin on his blog—but he loved my cello. I had worried about nothing."

"So it all came out well in the end," I said. Except for the second violin, of course.

"No," Victoria replied. "It did not all come out well in the end," she remarked, and there was that frown again. "After the label picked us up, he would drop in to see me, whenever he was in the States. Whenever he needed a favor. That was the true price of my folly. I might as well have bribed him; he was holding it over me either way. By then, I had already begun moving up through the ranks here at the Institute. I couldn't afford any bad publicity. So I complied. I did what I could when asked, most recently getting him a job at *Resounding Note*. I used to know the editor there."

Fleet nodded. He probably knew the editor there too. He knew everybody. "And then he dropped in at the banquet last night?"

"Yes, but he wasn't here to ask any favors. We didn't even speak. I'm not sure he recognized me."

"That hardly seems likely, does it?"

"I wouldn't have thought so either, but who knows how many people he might have had under his thumb. I could have been one of thousands, a face in a crowd."

There was that phrase again. Not the face one, the under-his-thumb one. Hutton had described Chet's power that way, and here was Victoria doing it herself. The man had a reputation.

"Well, it's a lovely face," said Fleet, standing. I'm constantly amazed how he can make statements like that and no one objects. It must be how he says it.

Victoria continued her plea. "You have to believe me, Ef; I had nothing to do with the murder. I know how it looks."

Fleet knew. He also believed. "I'll pass along what you told me about knowing Chester Callas before tonight. You may have to alter your official statement. For now, that's all I'll pass along," he assured her.

And with that, he gave me the cue that we should be passing along ourselves.

It took me a minute to pick up on it. I was busy looking at a stack of pamphlets on the shelf behind me: pamphlets like the one I had seen under Victoria's desk last night. "These all from auctions?" I asked her.

"They are." She subscribed to all the major auction houses. "Why do you ask?"

"No reason."

Victoria maintained her gaze. "Interestingly enough," she said, "one of the brochures was on the floor when I came in this morning—June 2008—along with a pile of scattered paper clips. You wouldn't know anything about that, would you, Mr. Hathaway?"

I chuckled lightly. Know anything? When had I ever known anything?

I twirled around, bouncing off Fleet's manly vest. "Ha-ha," I added and skipped past him and out into the hallway.

That's the nice thing about Enescu Fleet—he rarely asks you to qualify your behavior. I guess when you're as eccentric as he is, the question wouldn't be sporting. That, and he was usually ten steps ahead of everyone, regardless.

We took to the cobblestone again. The path was completely deserted now, not a single napping troubadour to be seen. We plunked down on a park bench.

"Did you believe her?" I asked.

He did. "I wonder, though, if you noticed anything peculiar about her story?"

"Peculiar how?"

"Out of place."

I'd had enough of this routine. I was no good as his investigative straight man. "Don't tell me, the night of the fateful concert she left her clavier in her hotel room?"

"Not exactly, no."

I was glad. That would have been too much. "What is a clavier anyway? Is it anything like a clavicle?"

Fleet said it was not, and I nodded. If he didn't know, he didn't know. "So what was out of place in her statement?"

He leaned back and folded his hands on his stomach.

"When a person constructs a strong lie," he said, "all the details play in harmony. Weaker fabrications, however, leave behind holes in the melody. If you know what to listen for, these holes come across as chords most sour, immediately detectable."

I wasn't really following him. Were we still talking clavicles?

"Victoria said she attempted to bribe Chester Callas, correct?"

"Correct."

"With what? You heard her; she could barely afford to keep living as she was. How, then, could she afford to bribe anyone?"

I pondered this. "Maybe she had socked away a little—"

"Not enough to make a difference with a man like Callas. She's an intelligent woman; she would have known this."

"So you don't think she offered to bribe him?"

"I do, but with what?"

I considered the evidence. "Her womanly charms?"

"Possible, but doubtful. I don't see her throwing herself at him. According to her own statement, the offer he rejected became his leverage. An attempt at seduction would hardly have the legs, if you'll excuse the metaphor. Nor, for that matter, would an offer of money. She could always deny it, despite what she said about appearances. No, whatever she tried to give him was something much more precious, something that could be proven against her, whether Chester accepted it or not."

He stood, scanning the horizon. It seemed Hutton and Pixie had opted for the comfort of Lyle Pendleton's villa over nature's splendor. They obviously weren't meeting us out here.

"At least we can be assured of one thing in Victoria's favor," said Fleet as we walked.

I was glad to hear it. The way things were sounding, I wouldn't have given her odds on making it through the afternoon. "What's in her favor?"

"Of all our suspects, Victoria was the one guest Chester knew well. Had she killed him, he would have only had to name her."

I agreed. And a normal person would have done so. But if one could be certain of anything in this case, it was that Chester Callas didn't have normalcy on his side.

That being said, I didn't think Victoria did it. My money was still on Lyle Pendleton. Fleet seemed to have some bizarre reason for excluding him, but I couldn't let the man go. I felt I was onto something good. It was so clean, so easy.

He was the Chairman of the Board, for goodness sakes.

I continued to feel strong in my convictions as we wound our way around the park, past the gothic-looking college buildings and toward the Tudor-styled home at the top of the hill. I felt strongly about them as we let ourselves in the front door, Lyle's housekeeper having stepped out for something.

I was even feeling pretty strong as we crossed the marbled foyer, entered Lyle's well-appointed study, and discovered the last of the Pendletons draped out at the foot of a lavender sofa, the back of his fluffy head covered in blood.

Okay, so maybe I was wrong about him.

13 — Out of Key

As we moved deeper into the room, another human head, blond and wavy of hair, bobbed up from behind the sofa: Hutton kneeling over the body. Pixie was also there, lending her assistance by snuffling its foot.

I wondered which one of them did it. Pixie I could almost understand. I knew she could get pretty ornery if she didn't receive her refreshing beverage. Hutton, though, should have known better. My uncle's testimony had all but cleared him of the Callas murder, and here he was, in the thick of it again with another corpse. You have to learn to pace yourself with these things.

He stood as we entered and dusted off his white khakis. "He's dead," he said.

No one made a move for a second or two. Then Fleet picked up Pixie from the rug, eliciting a low growl from the fuzzy bundle. I could appreciate her protest. If there's one thing that irks an up-and-coming canine PI, it's getting airlifted out of the area during forensic analysis.

Fleet asked what happened.

Hutton explained that he had dropped in on Lyle after we parted outside the library. Once arrived, he found the chairman in conversation with Sergei Brodovitch, the pianist. They had their serious faces on. Eventually Sergei popped off, and Hutton asked Lyle about the Enescu score.

"He seemed confused, like he didn't know what I was talking about. Either that, or he didn't trust me. At any rate, we had hardly begun to thresh it out when he remembered he had left his old gramophone playing in his study. He excused himself while I waited in the kitchen and had another freshly baked scone."

This revelation made me sniff meaningfully: I knew there would be scones!

"Did you notice anything unusual?" Fleet asked him. "Anything out of place?" He was asking everyone that today.

Hutton shook his head. He could hear music playing as Lyle opened and closed the study door down the hall. That was about it.

"What kind of music?" I wondered.

"Something classical."

I said that narrowed it down a whole helluva lot.

"After a few minutes, I got tired of waiting and tapped on the door. No answer. I heard the music whisk off inside. I knocked again, listened and then turned the knob. Locked. I didn't have my pick kit with me, so I proceeded around the side of the house and tried the terrace. Pixie helped. The French doors were sitting wide open. Inside Lyle was sprawled out on the area rug, the turntable turning without a record."

So that's what I kept hearing. Over yonder the wheel spun, but play as it might, no music came out. Just the *phut-phut-phut* of the needle on the track.

I took a glance around the room. I had described the space as well appointed. You could add well looted to that word portrait. Louis XIV drawers were pulled out, end tables knocked about with their scrolled legs in the air, and velvet cushions rubbed roughly against the nap. Someone—probably not the housekeeper—had whizzed through with a none-too-gentle touch.

Swiveling back to where the body lay, it looked like Lyle had been swatted from behind with a blunt object, perhaps the French horn resting on the floor beside him. Poor old geezer. I had always liked him.

Closer examination revealed a marble pedestal attached to the French horn, transforming it into a kind of plaque or trophy. It was no doubt the marble that had packed most of the punch. I'm not sure if the winds section would have had the *oomph* otherwise.

A few feet from the trophy an old LP record was poking out from under Lyle's palm. (LP for Lyle Pendleton.) Fleet was gazing at this. With Pixie in one hand and a pen in the other, he knelt down and pried up the disc. Lyle must have been in the process of taking it off the turntable when the murderer struck.

"What does it say?" I asked.

"*Sinatra and Swingin' Brass.*"

I gave a sullen snort. An album that was funny on many levels.

"That's not what was playing before," Hutton insisted. He might not know much about music, but he could differentiate between lounge-room vocals and a chamber ensemble.

That was as far as our parlor discussion got for now. A rustling in the hallway signaled the return of the housekeeper from her errands. Fleet left to speak with her, also to phone the police, while Hutton and I presided over the body. We took turns holding the squirming mutt.

After a couple minutes of Pass the Hound, Hutton crept over to the desk.

On top of a pile of ruffled papers sat a locking drawer, torn out from its drawer hole. A screwdriver had been jammed into the lock.

He leaned over and peered inside. Empty. He turned and gazed out the window. "Now who's this?" he declared.

I joined him at the vista. A dark, chiseled man in a black suit and tie was standing on the path across from the house, peering up at us.

I recognized him right off. My visitor from the vestibule. The king of the overhanging banisters. In a word, the Romanian (if he was Romanian).

Wherever he hailed from, I wished to speak with him. And quick.

I thrust Pixie into Hutton's arms and dashed out the door. I had no time for explanations.

At first, my rapid advance bore no fruit; the man had vanished. The key to these situations, however, is never lose your cool, never assume anything is how it seems. I took a couple deep breaths and looked again. Thanks to a limited student body, and an even more limited number of them wandering around in suits and ties, I was able to spot our observer receding into a clump of bushes on the left. The hunt was on.

Hutton was out on the path with me now, but I still had no leisure to pause and discuss. I bolted past him, turning laterally as he attempted to hand off Pixie with the shovel toss. I raced up a set of concrete stairs and dove into the puckerbrush. Hutton trailed a step behind, somewhat encumbered with the Maltese (not to mention the open-toed sandals he insisted on wearing in the summer months). The chase didn't last long. From the shrubbery our prey led us up a hill, across a sun-dappled field, through a patch of willow trees and over the sun-dappled laps of two coeds studying Schenker theory. From there it was back down a hill and behind an alley. By then I had closed the gap between me and the runner so sufficiently that I could have reached out and touched him.

That's just what I did do: touched him. The tag had enough snap to it that it sent him lurching forward. His sudden lurch, with all my weight applied behind it, sent me lurching myself. We both overbalanced and landed in a heap alongside an idling school bus.

There were musical instrument cases stacked everywhere—it was like Howdy Doody's family crypt. Before I knew what was happening, the Romanian had taken up arms: a trombone was in his grasp. In one good slice, he had whacked me in the skull with the tuning slide.

I had stated earlier that wind instruments lack *oomph.* I would like to amend this. They possess plenty of *oomph,* especially the brass. I sailed back, hitting the concrete with a thud.

I lay there a moment, rubbing my forehead. I had never really cared for the trombone, and now I could see why. No subtlety.

I've often asked myself whether the Romanian would have finished the job at this point. It's possible. He had the trombone, all locked and loaded. All he had to do was swing.

As it happened, he wasn't given the opportunity. No sooner had he raised the instrument in the air, the sun glistening off its spit release, than a ferocious ball of fluff sprang to my rescue.

Using my spleen as a springboard, it bounded into the fray, seizing my assailant by the kneecap. When you're a dog Pixie's size, about all the seizing you're going to do is in the kneecap region. The Romanian let out a startled yell, perhaps in his native tongue, and made a halfhearted attempt to swat her aside. The trombone proved a weak reed to lean on for this. Shaped as it is, always telescoping and whatnot, it doesn't really lend itself to fighting off deranged Maltese. It's definitely more of an upper-body weapon.

Unequal to the challenge, he moved to retreat down the alley, only to find Hutton waiting. The Romanian took a swing at him too, but even there the bludgeon missed by a foot. Hutton always did have good reflexes, even in sandals. He dodged the next slash effortlessly as well, bobbing and weaving out of the path of the remaining hacks.

I could see the Romanian was tiring; his trombone was drooping noticeably. I have no doubt that Hutton would have sealed the deal here, had Pixie, caught up in the excitement of the thing, not charged once more into the mix, chomping my friend on the big toe.

He bounded back, yelping something in his own native tongue; the Romanian flung the trombone at them; and Pixie, outraged with these raw tactics, chomped Hutton's other toe.

The Romanian, not missing a beat, skipped around the other side of the bus, leaving Hutton to massage his tootsies.

He straightened back up. He was showing us what it meant to be a strong warrior. (Native tribes liked to call him Fights with Wounded Toe.)

He suggested he and Pixie circle around the front and cut the blighter off at the pass. I could give chase to the rear. I nodded and went.

Just not very far. I had hardly taken a step before a pair of beefy mitts grabbed me around the shoulders. I had been snared by Henry Pratt. He was in his band getup, epaulettes as far as the eye could see. I barely recognized him without the trilby.

"Easy does it, sport. Where's the fire?"

I squirmed to get past, but these drummers have an iron grip. I wasn't going anywhere.

"Cool it, daddy-o. You're all heated up."

"Get off!"

He obliged but not before twisting my tendons into a clef note.

"I think you sprained my spine," I said.

"Sorry, bud, sometimes I don't know my own strength." He peered down at his hands, wiggling the wrists at the stem. "I hope you didn't throw off my flexors. We got a gig in Scranton today."

His flexors looked fine to me. If anything, kneading my upper torso like a ball of dough had probably loosened them up.

He seemed to see reason in my argument. He attempted a few invisible drumbeats. "I hope you're right. Now what's this all about, sport?"

He had already called me "sport" once. He was slipping.

"I'm chasing a Romanian," I replied. I spoke plainly. It only went to show, I felt, that these things are susceptible to a ready explanation if you just took the time to listen for it.

Pratt wasn't taking the time. "You were doing who with a what now?"

"Romanian. Chasing."

I paused as the sound of a bus transmission cranked into gear.

"The man stealing your bus," I said.

Pratt rotated around. Together we watched as his band transport creaked up the alley and around the bend, with the Romanian at the wheel.

I could only shake my head at the Pendleton bandleader.

Let's see how well his flexors got him to Scranton now.

14 — Pianoforte

We spent the next chunk of our morning giving more statements to the police. I finished up first, having drawn my old pal, Sgt. 'Stache, from the detective drawer.

I had even less to tell him about Lyle than I did Chet. He took down what I had, which was next to nothing, and that was that. That stoic super-cop and I bid adieu.

I would miss him.

Hutton didn't get off quite so easy. The authorities wanted to linger over him awhile. I believe the technical term is *detained for questioning*.

It made sense when you thought about it. The way he had wandered off from the banquet, minutes before the fall, and then landed knee-deep in another murder not eighteen hours later, I probably would have detained him a bit myself.

Ironically, the testimony of my uncle, the congressman, could have confirmed his whereabouts last night in a snap, but thanks to my brilliant maneuvering—my gift for guile—what I couldn't confirm was the uncle himself. I had done such a good job helping him disassociate himself from the affair that he had disassociated himself right off the table. His secretary said he hadn't been in his office all morning, and he refused to return any of my calls. He had simply vanished. (Just what this investigation needed: another phantom.)

I left him a couple emails, explaining the situation, but other than a generic response thanking me for my support in the coming election, I had nothing.

I didn't like the way things were shaping up for Hutton, didn't like them one iota. Guys like him—proud, eccentric, prone to rubbing people against the grain—they don't do well under the hot lamp of a police inquiry. I was concerned he might balk at their questions, which I knew from personal experience only makes matters worse. It was a tough spot for him.

On the other hand—and I hated to admit this to myself—it felt good not to be the one suspected of murder for once. I mentioned this to Fleet as we kicked back on the rear terrace, and he agreed that I had endured my share of awkward moments with the cops lately.

"How's the housekeeper holding up?" I asked him.

"Better than you might expect. Lyle was not a warm man, and he did not instill warmth in those around him."

I could see that. "Had she anything to suggest for the investigation?"

Fleet replied in the negative. Other than asserting that her employer had been a cold fish in his dealings with the domestic staff, exacting when it came to the ritual of his evening meal, and a Scorpio, she couldn't tell us much about Dr. Pendleton. She had seen Sergei arrive on her way out, but they hadn't spoken. She never spoke much with the foreign ones. She hadn't seen anyone else; she didn't know anything else. She had bouillabaisse burning on the stove. (Evidently the dead man was not her only client at the Institute.)

Closing the book on the housekeeper, we moved on to the matter of the runaway bus. It had turned up about a mile away, abandoned, with no Romanian in sight. The cops were running fingerprints on both it and the infamous trombone. No one was holding their breath.

Fleet paused here to glance at his phone. He wasn't a huge user of the latest tech, but he was adept enough to observe when he had a text message or not. "Apparently your fiancée and my daughter are up and about and wondering where the hell we are."

"Took them long enough."

"If you want to meet up with them, I still have a few things to attend to inside."

I stood. "Is one of those things getting Hutton released?"

Fleet gave a slight frown, which was his way of saying yes. He wasn't his namesake's most ardent fan, but he wasn't about to let him go down for a murder he didn't commit. It wouldn't befit the name Enescu Fleet—either one of them.

This was all supposing that Hutton hadn't committed the murder, of course. But, seriously, I knew the man; he was my closest friend. I was certain he couldn't have done it, and I had to think Fleet was pretty certain too. You only had to look at it rationally: if Hutton hadn't killed Chester Callas, then why kill anyone? When it came to good murder fodder, everybody else would pale in comparison.

"It's not like they can pin a motive on him," I pointed out.

"No."

"And there's still our mysterious Romanian to consider."

"Yes."

"If he is Romanian."

"Indeed."

Now I was the one frowning. "You do believe there was a Romanian?"

Fleet said of course he believed it. "That trombone didn't whack you itself. We might as well assume a Romanian whacked as anyone."

I agreed that it fit the theme.

On the theme of themes, I had one last one to bring up, and then I really had to dash. I knew how women could get when they felt you'd run out on them. You should have heard Lesley the time I stepped next door to borrow something, got roped into a neighbor's poker game, and didn't return home for an hour and a half. Never heard the end of it. And it's not like that grease fire would have actually burned the kitchen down anyway.

"Funny how the album in Lyle's grip was a Sinatra," I said.

"Yes," he replied.

I was beginning to feel locked out here. Snubbed, for lack of a better word. The man could give me a peek—a tiny glimpse into the whirling gears. After the morning we had been through, I felt I rated that much.

"Well, do you think it ties into the Callas murder or not?"

Going by recent form, I expected a simple *yes* or *no* in response. I ended up getting my choice of either.

"Yes and no," he said.

I didn't bother to decipher this. "Odd how Hutton heard different music playing in the study. Different from the album we found with Lyle, I mean."

"Not really," said Fleet. "I expected it would be."

That about did it for me. I moved to shove off when he called me back. He held up Pixie's leash.

"You don't mind?"

Normally I would have. But the fact remained that the little tyke and I had fought shoulder to shoulder that morning. The least I could do was offer her a spot of air.

I took the leash, and together we strode off into the great open spaces, one of us tinkling on the grass a tad more than the other.

It was after one such tinkle break that I came across the girls sitting on the park bench.

The extra sleep had agreed with them. Ate was looking rosy-cheeked and bright, full of untapped energy; whereas Lesley—she always looked like a million dollars. (I would have said a million pounds, in honor of her British heritage, but the last time I told her that she asked me why, had she put on weight?)

As I hove up alongside, Pixie sprang onto their collective lap and proceeded to relate our morning adventures. The dead body, the back-alley brawl, the scones: she yipped about it all. I felt it lost a little in the translation. "And that's where Hutton is now," I concluded, filling in the details the yapper had omitted.

"They've arrested him?" Ate asked. I was pleased to see her rosy cheeks registering concern over the prospect. Perhaps romance between her and Hutton was not the lost cause we had thought it was.

"Not arrested, detained. Your father's on it. I'm sure he'll beat the rap."

"There's a rap? You didn't say anything about a rap."

Lesley agreed that it sounded more serious when you talked about raps.

"Figure of speech," I said. "They haven't charged him with anything. It just looks suspicious how he keeps popping up at the murder scene, that's all."

"But that's just Hutton," said Ate. "He likes to immerse himself in his work."

Lesley agreed that if there was a way to make an ass of yourself, especially around a dead body or two, then Hutton was your man.

Pixie concurred with this assessment. With a hearty nod, she jumped off the bench and began running sprints up and down the lawn.

"Is there anything we should do?" Ate wondered.

"Not really. Your dad's got it in hand." I paused here to step out of the leash. In the mutt's exuberance, the thing had become entwined around my right ankle. Hutton wasn't the only one dealing in (w)raps.

"In that case, why don't we do some investigating on our own," she offered, and I could see some of that untapped energy bubbling to the surface.

I didn't follow her. Nor, unless I misinterpreted those large, blinking eyes, did Lesley.

Ate nodded toward one of the more modern structures in the distance: the Rondo Auditorium. A dour-looking young man was entering through the side entrance.

Lesley saw all. Or at least she saw some. "Is that Sergei Brodovitch?" she asked.

"It is. Someone pointed him out to me last night. We should go question him."

I didn't know about *should*, but we certainly *could*. No doubt he had already received his share of questions from official channels this morning. A visit from a trio of amateurs might actually come as a refreshing change.

"What about the woofer?" I asked, now disentangling my left leg.

"What about her?"

"Can we take her inside with us?"

Ate said why not? Fleets like her had been saying *why not* to questions like that for centuries. I believe you can find the words imprinted on their family crest.

It didn't take us long to locate Sergei. We only had to follow the sound of tinkling ivories (the other kind of tinkling). Proceeding through a pair of metal doors and down a long, open staircase, we discovered him up on stage, banging out some haunting melody to an empty auditorium. He appeared to be practicing.

Seeing us approach, he continued to hammer out the tune with even more vigor, never missing a key, but with a force of execution that nearly knocked us into the first row. Pixie seemed to be enjoying the performance most of all, yapping along at the noisier parts.

Eventually the phenom brought the thing to a close and sat staring at us.

From a distance, Sergei Brodovitch had looked like a typical young Eastern European musician, quiet and determined and full of brooding passion. Up close, he looked like a typical young Eastern European musician, quiet and determined and full of brooding passion.

His hair was on a forward incline, short and straight and all glinty, this either from fervent piano keying or fervent hair gel. His eyes were dark and closely set, his teeth uniform but with a thin gap between the top two. He reminded me of an ink drawing come to life.

"Yes?" he asked. "What is it?"

"That was beautiful!" chortled my fiancée.

He bowed his glossy head. I didn't blame her for gushing over him. That fancy piano playing coupled with the Czech accent—it *was* a pretty dreamy combination.

Not that I noticed or anything.

"Rachmaninoff," he stated.

Lesley tittered at the suggestion. "I couldn't, really. I'm engaged to be married!"

"Rachmaninoff is the composer," explained Sergei Brodovitch.

Lesley said oh. She tittered again and looked in my direction. I didn't titter. I squinted. Pixie licked his knuckle. We all show our appreciation for the arts in our own way.

"Rachmaninoff's 'Rhapsody on a Theme of Paganini,' " he informed us.

So that's what it was. Another rhapsody. Those early twentieth-century composers: they loved their rhapsodies. They were a rhapsodic bunch alright.

"What is it you want?" he asked, and went back to the closely set stare.

Ate took the helm. Lesley was too busy simpering with Rach-mania, and I was too busy squinting at all her simpering. Pixie was busy sniffing at Sergei's other knuckle.

"You met with Lyle Pendleton this morning?" Ate asked.

"Yes?"

"What did you talk about?"

"That is not your concern."

"I bet it is," she retorted, the blood of the investigating Fleets pumping through her veins. "You heard he was murdered, didn't you?"

"Of course I hear of this! The police, they well acquaint me with this fact. I tell you what I tell them: I know nothing about it."

"Don't you want his killer caught?"

Sergei smacked the keys with a petulant fist.

"Of course I want killers caught! Dr. Pendleton, he was like the grandfather to me. More! This is all that I want, his killer brought to justice."

"Then help us. Right now the police are wasting their time grilling the wrong man."

"I know nothing about this grill," said Sergei. "I cannot help you." The pianist stood and slammed the lid shut on the keys. The way he banged about I was surprised he hadn't broken one of those magic fingers. "I must go."

Ate wasn't so easily put off. "Is it true that you're backed by the Czech mafia?" she called after him.

Sergei froze in the overhead lights.

I could see why. It's not the sort of question you get asked all that often. I almost never get asked it.

"What is this you say?"

I was right there with him. *What was it she said?*

I stepped closer and whispered, "Where are you going with this?"

She whispered back, "I couldn't sleep last night, so I read up on everybody. There's this rumor that Sergei is backed by the Czech mafia. Just go with it."

"Go with what?"

"Go with it and see," she whispered, and I whispered *gotcha.* Go with it. I could do that.

"They say Sinatra had mob ties too," whispered Lesley, also going with it.

"What is this now?" Sergei repeated, not going with it or whispering.

"The Czech mob," spoke up Ate. "Is that what you and Lyle argued about? Did he discover your underworld connections? Is that why you pretended to leave and then came back in the study and bonked him?"

Sergei made an impatient gesture. "We did not argue. I do not bonk. He was the good man, Lyle Pendleton. You should not say these things!"

"Then it's not true?"

"What is not?"

"You're not connected to the Czech mob?"

"What is this connected? I know nothing of Czech mob. What are these lies? Who told you these?"

"Twitter."

"He is a liar, this Twitter. I do not have to listen to this!"

He spun around, nearly colliding with me in his attempt to flounce off. I was holding Pixie. Neither of us was amused.

"Pah!" he said, and I said pah right back. (I bet he didn't expect me to know any Czech.)

At the risk of coming off like Henry Pratt, I gave him my best flinty stare. "Easy does it there, friend," I added. "The lady hasn't finished her questions."

I probably should have left it with the flinty stare. But you know how it is. Girls watching—you want to appear cool.

I reached out and gripped his arm. Just a little something to keep him with us and show him who's boss.

Apparently it wasn't me. He slapped my grip aside like it was a second-rate piano lid. When I tried to reattach, he stiff-armed my right shoulder so firmly that I almost pulled a Chester Callas falling off the stage—which probably wouldn't have done Pixie any good at all.

I recovered at the last moment, the back of my heels teetering on the brink. I stood there rubbing my ouchy spot as he stormed off, muttering to himself.

These musicians, they're all tough guys.

15 — An Underlying Harmony

Nearly getting my shoulder dislocated by another promising young performer had done nothing to improve my mood on the walk back to Lyle's villa.

Properly considered, I should have felt like a regular Pendleton prince, strolling along with two pretty girls at my side—three, if you included the one snuffling pinecones. Instead, I felt shaky and unwell, as if I had recently avoided taking a reverse grand jeté onto my head. I wasn't convinced that we had made any progress in our murder investigations; I was concerned that Hutton was still languishing in police custody; and I was fairly certain that my fiancée had become infatuated with a steely eyed virtuoso who may or may not have ties to the Czech underworld. It was enough to distract any man from princely emotions.

I was glad to see that Ate, at least, shared my views. On the investigation anyway.

"That could have gone better," she sighed, untying her hair from its ponytail. She had pulled it back during her one-woman third degree-ing, but now she let it all hang out. "I probably could have played it closer to the vest."

I didn't think she had done so bad for her first time. And it wasn't like Lesley or I lent that much to the mix.

"Mmm," agreed Lesley, still mooning over the dreamboat that was Sergei Brodovitch.

"I thought I had him right where I wanted him with that Czech business."

I knew how she felt. I had thought I had Lyle Pendleton right where I wanted him too, and then he had to go and make himself the next murder victim. Sneaky bastard.

"There was even a Sinatra connection," she said, and there I had to question her reasoning. I still wasn't sold on that one.

"Was there?" I asked.

"Wasn't there?" she replied.

"Mmm," said Lesley.

Ate and I blinked at her. Ate continued:

"They're both musicians with mob ties. It was as good as that chairman of the board thing of yours."

"Was it?" I retorted.

"Wasn't it?" she remarked.

"Ever thought about taking up the piano, Johnny?" Lesley asked.

I turned back to Ate. "I'm not saying there isn't a connection, but is that how Chester would have identified Sergei? Frank Sinatra?"

"He might."

"Why? If he knew about his affiliations, wouldn't he have also known his name?"

"I suppose."

"Of course he would, and that's what doesn't make sense. He would have just said it. It's the same conclusion we arrived at with Victoria Walters. Even if he didn't know Sergei's name, or couldn't remember it, there are tons of better methods for communicating his identity."

"Like what?"

"I don't know. He was probably the only Czech in the audience."

"What difference could it make if there was another Chet in the audience?"

"Not *Chet*. *Czech*. Sergei was the only *Czech*, so *Chet* could have used this quality of *Czech* to identify him. *Chet* could have."

"You're making my head throb. What if he didn't realize he was *Czech*? *Chet* didn't?"

"Then he could have said something like 'head piano guy'; that might have worked."

"Or rugged good looks," offered Lesley.

"Exactly. The mob stuff is too obscure," I argued. "Cryptic."

"Maybe you're right," said Ate.

"Of course I am. We keep landing in this trap. The Sinatra Snare. We look for Sinatra, and Sinatra is all we see."

We had reached Lyle's villa. From the number of cop cars still disfiguring the driveway, the grill looked as hot as ever.

"So who do you think did it?" Lesley asked me. It was the first non-Sergei comment she had expressed in the last ten minutes, and it took me off guard.

"Hopefully not the man the police do," I replied.

And in the four of us went.

The first person we encountered inside was Enescu Fleet. He greeted us with his customary half-smile and twinkling eyes, not forgetting to include Pixie in his salutations—picking the little wiggler up off the tile and tousling her fur.

"How's everyone doing?" he asked.

"How's Hutton doing?" Ate asked him.

I was touched. Her continued interest in the welfare of a man, who as recently as twelve hours ago, trailed all long shots for a crack at her affection, was a true inspiration. I'm not sure Lesley would have looked on my confinement with such womanly compassion. I should think *This is what my parents warned me about* the likely sentiment, winning out over *What has he gotten himself into now?* and (hopefully) *I wonder if Sergei offers piano lessons in the tub?*

"Is he still in with the police?" Ate asked.

Fleet gave his daughter a soulful nod. The authorities had made the kitchen their interrogation room, and no, nobody had come out yet.

She glowered. "Haven't you talked to them? Where's that famous Enescu Fleet charm?"

"I was just about to exercise it. I only got back myself a few minutes ago."

"Got back? Got back from where?"

I didn't blame her for her chagrin. What could be more important than setting the record straight on our friend Hutton?

"I had a few errands to make," he explained.

"What kind of errands?" demanded his daughter.

"Meeting with the coroner, for one."

Ate and I rolled our eyes.

It was my turn to voice a critique. Ate had talked herself out for a while, and Lesley was checking her makeup in the hall mirror. I had the floor. "What could the coroner tell you about Lyle that you couldn't observe for yourself? He was bashed in the head with a French horn; what else is there to say?"

"Not Lyle, Johnny—Chester. I met with the coroner about Chester Callas."

I rolled my eyes a second time. Chester Callas. That murder was so last night.

Ate found her second wind. "Dad, you need to do something."

"On my way now, honey," he said. He observed our tiny procession on the march with him.

"I'm coming along," said Ate. How she thought she was going to persuade the authorities of Hutton's innocence, I didn't know, but I admired her pluckiness.

"I'll come too," I suggested. The more the merrier.

"Sure, whatever," said Lesley, joining the horde.

We headed down the hall and pushed through the swinging kitchen door.

I don't know what we expected to find. Hutton flopped back against a hard metal chair, sweat dripping down from his forehead… Perhaps some hulking police sergeant hunched over him, brandishing brass knuckles…

What we didn't expect was Hutton standing in front of a whiteboard with one of those long pointer thingies in his hand: not a single hard chair, hot light or knuckle-duster on the horizon.

There were Pendleton schematics tacked up on the wall, police sketches of a man holding a trombone alongside these, and several football-style strategy doodles on the whiteboard. Somehow, in some way, Hutton was running point on the investigation, and I couldn't fathom why.

As we came more into the kitchen, I heard him say something to one of the sergeants (not hulking or hunching) about checking the garages again. He then paused to accept a cup of tea from another. He thanked the man briefly, sipped and gave the thumbs-up to a rotund woman stirring a gray-speckled pot on the back stove.

"Not too much sugar this time, Mr. H?" asked the late Dr. Pendleton's housekeeper.

"Just perfect, Alma," said Hutton.

I didn't know what to say. Wait—yes, I did. "What the—"

"Fig roll," proffered Alma, appearing at our side. She was holding a plate of pastries. With her employer murdered, they were just going to go to waste otherwise.

I took one without nuts and continued my inquiry. "What the—"

"I thought I would help out," said Hutton, waving his men out the door as we ushered him aside.

"*You* help?" echoed Lesley.

"Absolutely. Once we got things straightened out regarding those pesky alibis, I placed myself at their service."

It looked more like they were at his service, if you asked me. "But how—? Why—?"

"Shared resources, Hath. I'd already memorized the layout of the campus when I was out walking Pixie, so naturally I had a few thoughts on where our trombone-wielding assailant might be concealing himself. They were happy to canvass my views."

"*Your* views?" echoed Lesley.

"Of course. These fellows know an authoritative voice when they hear one. Also, I might have implied that my previous experience could prove invaluable to them."

"What previous experience?" I asked.

"Oh, you know. My cases in Europe, Canada. My work for the crown."

"You worked for Crown Royal," I said, "helping weed out a counterfeit-whisky-bottle ring."

"Yes, well, it would appear that all they heard was *crown*. I may have also mentioned how I assisted in tracking down the Palm Beach Poisoner a few years back."

"I tracked down the Palm Beach Poisoner," said Enescu Fleet.

"Yes, I know. But I describe it so much better than you do, don't I? Besides, one Fleet is pretty much as good as another, isn't it?"

"No."

"Right. Well, anyway, what really turned the scale was the captain learning that I had been at school with his son. His wife's English, you know."

"What son?" I wondered.

"Who knows? Bob, Tom, Fauntleroy—who can remember? The point is, the captain could hardly throw the book at one of his kin's oldest school chums. Not when one of our oldest classmates was the first murder victim last night."

I harrumphed. I'd gone to that school too. I should have been the one doodling on whiteboards and having tea made without too much sugar. I took a sullen bite of fig roll.

I couldn't help noticing Ate hadn't said anything since we entered Hutton's wheelhouse. I glanced at her just as her ruby lips were parting in a sneer. "We were worried about you, you know," she growled and, turning on her heel, left the room.

"What's eating her?" Hutton asked.

I really couldn't say. Maybe she didn't like fig rolls.

Now that Hutton was free to go, we could continue on to our next investigative destination, and we could do it as one close-knit unit.

Well, maybe not all that *knit*. After her flounce from Lyle's villa, Ate was making good time plodding up the path ahead of us. She wanted to be alone. Lesley had joined her, because when women say they want to be alone they, of course, mean with other women. Hutton was on Pixie duty again, catering to the animal's every whim about twenty yards behind. Fleet and I were somewhere in the middle.

I took the opportunity to pry deeper into those errands of his. I've found, from close association with the man, that the more you can learn about his offstage activities, the less baffled you'll be when he eventually ties everything together.

"You were gone a goodly while. You must have done more than speak with the coroner?"

"I did. Although what the coroner had to tell me was worth the price of admission."

"Oh yeah? What did the coroner have to tell you?"

"Chester's cause of death."

I held back another sigh. We'd been over all this. "You said he died from a knife wound."

"The knife wound did not kill him."

"Ah. Then it was the fall, after all?"

"No, not the fall either."

I was feeling baffled again, earlier than usual. "Then what?"

"Chester Callas was poisoned."

There was a short pause, made up of me staring, and then Fleet proceeded:

"The exact name of the toxin wouldn't interest you, I'm sure, but I can tell you that it is exceedingly difficult to trace. It mimics a severe allergic reaction. The coroner might never have discovered it had it not been for the knife wound. It made him conduct a more thorough examination of the body."

I was amazed. Stabbed, shoved from a great height, poisoned. One wonders why nobody took a potshot at him as he plummeted to the table.

Poor old Chet. Even Rasputin got a bracing dip in the river for his trouble.

As fascinating as this all was—and it was pretty fascinating—I still wanted to know how Fleet had spent the rest of his morning. I had a notion that there was gold in them thar errands.

"So after the coroner's office, you went—?"

He stood holding the door for me. We had moved so briskly keeping time with Ate that we had arrived at the Pendleton Library in record time. (Apparently the library was our next destination.)

He blinked at me. "What's that? After the coroner? Later, Johnny, later. Right now we need to see if Nate Goody is in. There's something I want to talk to him about."

16 — Signature Tune

Inside, the Pendleton Library had pretty much returned to normal. Crime-scene photographers had given way to shaggily dressed scholars; police-tape barriers had been torn down in favor of cubicles stacked with hefty tomes. Everything was status quo again. On the surface anyway.

Status quo was anything but what Hutton's reputation was. Not twenty minutes had elapsed since we left Lyle's villa, and already rumors had begun to swirl surrounding the great investigative consultant with the cool black rims and wavy blond hair. The young Enescu Fleet was the talk of the Pendleton.

There were furtive whispers as we filed down the corridor, surreptitious looks as we navigated the cubicles in the main library, and more than one student, hoping to appear *with it*, shot him an up-nod as we made our way to the administrative offices. Quietly and steadily the campus was abuzz with the man.

Perhaps he was the true Pendleton Prince, after all.

For as long as I had known him, Hutton had taken this approach. Bold, frenetic. Compared with Ate's father, who embraced dignity over pageantry, he preferred to bound on the scene like a rabid caribou—fascinating the participants with his avant-garde style and refreshing outlook. This would go on for about an hour, until he burned himself out. It's all about pacing.

Even still, these runs of his were impressive while they lasted, and this afternoon was no exception. Not only had his avant-garde-ness earned him his freedom, the cops' trust and three cups of tea; but a passing library volunteer, sensing that we might have some trouble with the sixth member of our party, offered to take Pixie off our hands while we met with Dean Goody. You can't buy service like that. Although, I believe Hutton did tip her (unless he was giving her his gum to throw away).

With Enescu Fleet leading the cavalcade—the original, un-transcribed Fleet—the five of us headed around the corner and crowded into Nate Goody's office.

The dean was already playing to capacity. Nate was on the phone, grunting occasional monosyllables into the receiver. Tanya Saxon was standing at the wall of photos. Victoria Walters was on Nate's peculiar sofa again, her eyes moist with either the news of Lyle Pendleton's murder or all the animal hair that went into that furniture's construction.

Fleet addressed himself to Victoria first. I couldn't hear what he said, mostly because I had edged away, pretending to check email on my phone. (I'm no good in these situations.) Whatever he told her, it was likely better than "There, there," which is what I would have said had I been called upon to speak.

She looked up and smiled, dabbing her eyes. "I don't know why I'm so upset. Lyle Pendleton was a sour old bastard in many ways. And I don't think he liked me. In fact, I know he didn't. And yet, somehow, that makes it all worse somehow, doesn't it?" she asked, and Fleet nodded and said he understood. I was glad somebody did.

The Fleet-Walters contingent was clearly out of my league. I backed slowly away.

The Hutton-Ate-Lesley conglomerate, in the interim, had shifted over to the picture window behind Nate Goody's desk. Hutton was pretending to identify some breed of butterfly on the sill while the ladies were pretending to care.

I toyed with joining them but wasn't really up for one of Hutton's fake seminars. They're frequently informative, but I never seem to pass the pop quizzes.

That left Tanya Saxon.

I meandered over to where she stood and hoped she didn't want to talk about the murders, Lyle Pendleton's legacy or the hole in my blue jeans.

For the first blissful minute, she didn't. All that could be heard was the sound of Nate's grunts, Fleet and Victoria's modulated voices and Hutton discussing larvae.

It wasn't too bad: just me, the grande dame and a wall of old photos.

In light of his murder, I expected to find her looking at pictures of the youthful Lyle, but she wasn't. She was looking at pictures of the youthful Tanya.

"Would you believe I was beautiful once, Mr. Hathaway?"

I hate it when women ask me questions like that. There's no appropriate reply. *Yes*, *no*, *pass*—they all have their relative merits and drawbacks.

"No" seemed a bit harsh, while "Yes" implied a certain level of familiarity I wasn't comfortable unfurling around a much older woman.

I passed. I said, "Ha-ha," whatever that was supposed to mean, and that seemed to cover it for now.

We gazed at the pics in silence. (Not that it matters, but she was pretty hot in her youth.)

What amazed me even more than her unexpected youth and beauty was the fact that she had apparently once been crowned Miss Hoboken. One of the photos showed her in her sash, alongside a youthful yet still sour Lyle Pendleton, both of them cast in the circular shadow of a very young Nate Goody. The words across her chest were unmistakable. Miss Hoboken. She didn't look like someone from Hoboken.

Thankfully, Nate hung up with his call before good manners compelled me to inquire what her special talent had been, and whether contestants in the late 1800s had to flirt with the judges.

We could finally get around to the purpose of our visit. Not that I knew what this was either.

The dean apologized for keeping us. "The trustees and special alumni won't let up. Pester, pester, pester. You would think I had done the murders myself."

It wasn't the most tactful remark he could make, but something I had noticed about Nate was he wasn't the most tactful fellow around.

"Of course it's a tragedy," he said, rising out of his self-preoccupation. "Lyle's murder. It was a tragedy. And Callas too," he added. Evidently, even long-haired British bores had a special place in Nate's heart. He heaved a full-bodied sigh. "I suppose we shall have to shut down the Institute until the police have finished their investigations."

I could tell Victoria Walters differed with this assessment. She looked up, dabbed twice, but otherwise made no contribution to the discussion.

The younger folks (Hutton, Lesley, Ate and I) also said nothing. Apparently Hutton realized that this was not the place for his refreshing outlook. Lesley and Ate might have voiced an opinion, I think, had Lesley's short skirt and Ate's belly revealing T-shirt not made them feel like a couple of harlots in Tanya Saxon's presence. Or so they later told me. They should have seen her in her Miss Hoboken sash.

I, on the other hand, couldn't care less what the nibs did with their institute. Close the campus; don't close it—it mattered not. I leaned toward closing it, at least the dorms. It might mean I would actually get a decent night's sleep that week.

"You well know," said Tanya Saxon, "that we cannot close the Institute."

Nate knew nothing of the sort. "Why not? There are hardly any students on campus, and we can push back what classes we do have until next week."

"It's not the students I'm concerned with," said Tanya, and I didn't blame her. She hadn't been a student herself for eighty years. "This is the Pendleton's busy season for cultural events. There are nine concerts planned this weekend alone. Rachel Pine's sold-out Paganini, as a case in point, is scheduled to begin in less than an hour. The guests have already begun arriving."

"Yes, but—"

"We can't afford to turn them away."

The dean had started *yes-but*-ing again, when Victoria chimed in in support of Tanya's claim. "Dr. Saxon's right. We can't close. I *do* care about the students, and we can't deny them their education."

"Nor you your debut performance on Sunday," said Tanya tartly.

"I wasn't even thinking of that," replied Victoria, equally tart, and I came within inches of saying, "Ladies, ladies, let's not argue." I didn't—I had no death wish—but I did try and convey a "Ladies, ladies"-like wrinkle to my brow. I'm not sure anyone noticed it.

Nate also made no attempt to *lady, lady* them. He did, however, sputter ineffectually and look puff-faced. "Nobody's suggesting we deny anyone anything!" he spouted. "We simply postpone. We put off classes for a few days, postpone the concerts, and let the police work. Rachel Pine will understand. And now that you mention it, I'm not sure they will need days. No offense intended to Mr. Fleet, but I understand that the authorities have brought in a special consultant. An expert on loan from Scotland Yard or somewhere. From what I understand, he has already begun to make great progress in the case."

Hutton had cleared his throat on the phrase "special consultant." He cleared it again now. "That would be me," he said.

Nate glared at him. "What would?"

"I'm the special consultant on loan from—well, it's not important where I'm on loan from," said Hutton. "The point is, I'm all yours until this case is solved."

Nate continued to glare at him, wondering what madness this was. "Who are you?"

"Just another Enescu Fleet here to help."

"You're Enescu Fleet?"

"One of a pair, yes. Not available in stores. Think of us as a collector's item, more valuable when sold together."

Nate had no desire to think of them in any such way. "You're the special consultant?"

"None specialer."

"Then what are you doing in here? Why aren't you out there consulting?"

Hutton replied that he was. Not outwardly—inwardly. Always consulting. Even when you didn't think he was, he was consulting away. It's all in the mind, consulting.

A moment passed in stunned silence. Then the room erupted with renewed fervor. Nate said he had no choice but to shut the doors and postpone. Tanya stated unequivocally that rescheduling the concerts was out of the question. Victoria argued that many of the students had nowhere else to go. That's why they were here now.

Listening to the ladies, you never would have guessed that they were essentially agreeing with each other.

Nate probably wouldn't have guessed it. He slipped off his giant glasses and rubbed his giant, puffy face. "We appear to have reached an impasse."

"Not necessarily," said Enescu Fleet.

It was nice to hear from him again. I didn't really believe that the "special consultant" crack had given offense, as Nate Goody thought it might, but you never knew when our aged leader might decide to sit one out, regardless.

He sat out no longer. He stood and addressed the room:

"I don't think there's any danger to the students or those visiting the Institute."

"Hear, hear," said Tanya Saxon. She was a fiery old bird.

"I think you're right," muttered Victoria Walters.

I thought she might have shown more passion. You're an orchestral director now, I might have told her. Go bold, like my friend Hutton, not soft and subdued. Think Bruckner, not Debussy.

Fleet continued, "The murders committed on campus were not random acts of violence. The culprit had specific targets within the organization. It doesn't involve the public."

"I agree," said Special Consultant Hutton. "I'd stake the reputation of Enescu Fleet on it." He didn't mention which Enescu Fleet.

"You both sound like you know who this culprit is," Tanya commented.

They decided to play it cagey. Hutton stuck out his bottom lip in thought as Fleet resumed his speech. "Am I correct that the last words spoken by Chester Callas yesterday evening are known by everyone here?"

No one replied, so it would seem he was correct.

"Frank Sinatra," said Enescu Fleet. "We are operating under the theory that that name forms the basis of a dying clue. A pointer to the identity of the killer."

"But what could it mean?" Victoria asked.

"We've had some theories on that too. None have panned out. Not until Lyle Pendleton was killed, that is."

Tanya Saxon was gazing at him. "Don't tell me Lyle mentioned Mr. Sinatra too?"

"No. Lyle mentioned nothing. He was already dead when Hutton found him. But he didn't have to speak. His hand was lying on an old LP album. *Sinatra and Swingin' Brass.*"

It went over well. Nate Goody sputtered "By golly"; Victoria gasped; and Tanya slowly shook her tightly coifed head, as if to say this wasn't how things worked back in Hoboken.

Fleet turned to the Dean of Pendleton. "Do you know what the first song is on *Sinatra and Swingin' Brass*, Nate?"

Nate had no idea. "What is it?"

" 'Goody Goody.' "

Nate Goody gaped. "Goody—"

"—Goody," concluded Fleet. "Perhaps you would like to try that on for size."

17 — A Clash of Symbols

This went over even better. Tanya Saxon closed her eyes and looked faint; Victoria said "Oh dear"; and Nate burbled, "But I, what, how—" Suffice it to say, Fleet had his audience right where he wanted them.

Even the peanut gallery, made up of myself and the other youngsters, stared wide-eyed.

Fleet went on, bearing down on Nate like a bearded barbell, "You told a roomful of people yesterday that Chester Callas was here to perform a transcription of Enescu's third Romanian Rhapsody. You said he discovered the score himself. Those were lies, weren't they?"

"I, well—"

"Chester never had any such score. He came here because he thought you had it."

"Well, I—"

"You lured him here to die."

"Yes, I invited him here. That part is correct. But I didn't kill anybody."

"There never was any score, was there?"

"Not as such, no. We thought we had one, Lyle and I, but it turned out to be a hoax."

"But you didn't need an actual manuscript to draw Chester into your web."

"No. I mean, yes. I mean, I didn't have a web," said Nate Goody.

"You deny deceiving him?"

"Yes. I mean, no. I deceived him," Nate admitted. "We brought him here under false pretenses—that part is true—but I did it to embarrass him, not to kill him."

"Perhaps you would care to qualify that," said Fleet.

Nate said he would. He swallowed thrice and looked like he could use a quick dram of Romanian tuica to steady his nerves. "I hated him. I don't deny that."

"Why did you hate him?"

"Because of a violin. Not just any violin. A Guarneri. You remember it, don't you, Victoria?"

Victoria gave a solemn nod and said she remembered it.

"This was in the spring of 2008. March, I believe. I was over in England on a matter concerning the estate of one of my distant relatives, and she was there working out a record deal. She had been one of my students back in the old days, and we decided to catch up. I probably mentioned the violin to you over lunch one afternoon."

Victoria nodded again. It was probably over lunch, she agreed, yes.

"I had just inherited the Guarneri, you see," said Nate. "Only, I didn't know it was a Guarneri then. Violins never have been my forte. I just knew it was old. Victoria recommended an appraiser she knew in the States, but before I could get in touch with him I was contacted by someone in England. Chester Callas. I have no idea how he heard about the instrument, but he seemed very well informed. He told me his family had been appraisers and he could get me a splendid deal. He fed me a bunch of rubbish about the difficulty in transporting a commodity such as that, some other nonsense about saving me VAT, which I still don't quite understand, and all in all talked such a good game that I sold it to him. Only—"

"Only you sold it to him for a bargain. And before you knew where you were, he had turned around and sold it himself for about a zillion times the price."

When you think of bold and manly statements such as these, you probably think of Enescu Fleet. Or maybe Hutton.

'Twasn't them. This bold and manly statement was pure Hathaway. It was probably my first successful deduction, and I will always cherish it as such.

The moment I spoke it, Nate Goody shimmied from flabby head to argyle sock. "Why yes," he bleated, "that's exactly correct." He looked even more in need of that tuica than before.

I thought Hutton's revelation as special consultant had stunned the room. It had nothing on mine.

Hutton, Ate and Lesley eclipsed all other wide-eyed stares. Victoria's blue peepers shone with brightly lit astonishment, whereas Tanya Saxon held up just short of saying, "Why, I'll be. All this time I thought the young man was an idiot!"

Even Fleet beamed like a proud father. "Well done, Johnny. You're a step ahead of me. How did you work that out?"

I waved an airy hand. I preferred not to dwell on specifics. The mention of a violin, the 2008 date—it all seemed to fit with the auction brochure I had seen in Victoria's office. Offhand, I can't say how I connected all the parts. It just sort of came to me, and I blurted it out.

Obviously what had happened was this: after the murder, Nate had wandered by Victoria's bookshelf. Pawing through her old brochures, he had sat at her desk with the relevant auction in hand, brooding on what he had done to Callas and why.

"So Chet did you down on this auction business, and you killed him for it."

My moment as stunning deducer had come to a close. Nate scowled and grunted, "No, that's not it at all. I already told you; I didn't kill anybody."

I said oh. He had told us that; he was right. I sat back down, and Fleet carried on:

"If not murder, then what motivated you to bring him here?"

Nate's hauteur deflated. "I told you; I was just trying to embarrass him, get back at him. I had my department get in touch with him and tell him about the score we thought we had found. We asked him here to help verify it. Only, the night of the banquet, I made out like he had it all along and was going to perform it for us."

"We remember, Nate. We were there."

"So you were. Anyway, that was the motivation. He would have to stand up in front of a roomful of his peers and admit that he had no score, he wasn't going to perform anything, and he had no idea what was going on. He would look like, well, a fool; that's what he would look like. Either that or he would storm out without saying a word, and that would make him look even more the fool."

The room sat absorbing this—led by Fleet, who was actually standing. It was a specious explanation to be sure and not an easy one to refute. But if anyone could knock a specious explanation on its ass, it was he.

"And the murder?" he said.

"I was as shocked as anyone by that."

"Chester's or Lyle's?"

"Both of them! How could anyone think that I could harm Lyle Pendleton? The man and I were practically family. We've known each other our whole lives. You don't bludgeon someone you've known since childhood."

I peered over at Hutton, a man I had also known since childhood, and considered this another specious argument.

Nate pulled himself up in his chair, no easy task with that potato-shaped head of his. "You might think I had something to do with the Callas murder. I didn't, but you're free to think what you will. But I refuse to sit here and be accused of killing Lyle Pendleton. I would never lay a hand on my old friend."

"Of course you wouldn't," said Fleet, and half the room looked at each other in confusion. I was in the confused half.

"You believe I'm innocent?" asked Nate, slouching in disbelief.

"Of Lyle's murder? I do. I believe the clue was planted. And if it was, it's unlikely you planted it to incriminate yourself."

"Right," said Nate, nodding. "I mean, huh?"

"There's no way Lyle could have secured that clue at the time of his murder," explained Enescu Fleet, sounding like Chester Callas criticizing our previous cases.

"Why not?" asked the dean, gaping again.

"Lyle was struck from behind. His killer sneaked up on him. Why, then, would Lyle have selected that particular album? Either he knew his life was in danger, in which case he never would have turned his back on his would-be killer; or he was none the wiser, and, therefore, would not have had the wherewithal to grab the clue."

"Couldn't Dr. Pendleton have selected the clue after he was struck?" Lesley asked.

Nate shot her another angry glare, no doubt asking himself who invited this one?

Fleet didn't believe so. "According to witness accounts, there was another record playing just prior to the murder. For the reasons I just mentioned, I don't think Lyle could have returned this to his collection and still selected the telling album. Had the killer returned it, he or she would have most certainly returned the *Goody Goody* album as well, unless the killer was *not* Nate. The only reason to leave it would be to lay the blame on the dean. So it was a plant."

Nate appeared vindicated. "I told you I couldn't have done it."

"Killed Lyle?" qualified Fleet. "No. Not unless you left the clue as a double bluff. But somehow I doubt you would have been that clever."

"Exactly," Nate concurred. "I mean, what?"

"But that doesn't let you off the hook for Callas."

"No?" wondered the dean. "No, I suppose it doesn't," he grumbled. "I didn't kill him, you know."

"Maybe not, but perhaps you would care to shed some light on how everyone learned about Chester's last words. Clearly they're known, or else Lyle's killer never would have thought to plant the false lead. It was you who let the cat out of the bag, wasn't it, Nate?"

"Well—"

"You might as well come clean," said Tanya Saxon. "Buck up, man. No sense in remaining coy."

Nate spared us that. He bucked up as directed. "I wear a hearing aid," he confessed. "It's quite a good one. If I adjust it just so"—he adjusted it just so—"I can hear everything anyone says fifty yards away."

"You eavesdropping old crump!" muttered Lesley. That's my fiancée, folks.

"I never really mean to listen in," said the eavesdropping old crump. "I just can't help myself sometimes."

Fleet understood. Some men drink, others gamble; Dean Goody listened. "And when Chester fell—"

"I had to know what he said. Wouldn't you have?"

Fleet agreed he probably would. But then again, he was curiouser than most. "How many have you told about this?"

"About the last words? Oh, not that many. My secretary. Lyle. Tanya. Victoria. Henry Pratt."

Hutton and I shared a significant glance. Good old Henry. Now that we knew that Henry Pratt was in the loop, I had to ask myself: did Nate tell him *about* Frank Sinatra, or did he tell him to *be* Frank Sinatra?

"Does he always talk like that?" I said.

Nate twisted around to look at me. "Like what?"

"Like he's just come in from a night on the town with Peter Lawford."

Nate considered the question. He never really thought about it. He wasn't sure.

"Why exactly did you mention it to Mr. Pratt?" Fleet tacked on.

They were coming over the plate a bit fast for the dean now. He wasn't sure. He never thought about it. "I guess it just seemed natural. Henry was Lyle's and my right-hand man on the missing rhapsody. He's the one who originally helped locate what turned out to be a fake, and when he learned Callas was coming, I might have let something slip about my prank."

"And what about Lyle? He must have known about that too?"

"No, nobody did. I left the announcement as a surprise. After the murder, Lyle figured out what I'd done and didn't approve, but by then we had other things to concern ourselves with."

Fleet said, "I see."

The phone on Nate's desk buzzed. His secretary came on the speaker, telling her employer that several members of the board had arrived and wanted to talk about electing a new chairman. They were awaiting him in the conference room.

Nate muttered something about vultures. "You might as well join us, Drs.," he told Victoria and Tanya, and the pair nodded and moved to exit.

Fleet held Victoria at the door. "Just so you know, Lyle thought very highly of you. He told me he could think of no one better qualified to assume the role of Pendleton orchestral director."

Victoria opened her mouth to reply, had no words and left smiling.

Hutton, Ate and Lesley followed: Ate saying that she had a thought on the case and Hutton saying that was interesting, because he had a couple thoughts himself. Lesley silenced them both, whispering, "Shush, the old cyborg might hear us."

Fleet and I went last. I had just reached the door when I looked back and saw the old cyborg had detained Fleet.

Lingering behind, just to make sure no one hit anyone in the head with any marble horns, I was surprised to see Nate all atwitter. He was a man of many moods, the dean.

"Now that they're gone, I can tell you what I've been itching to say for the last hour."

"And what is that?" asked Fleet.

Nate escorted us away from the door. You could never be sure who might be aiming a highly tuned hearing aid at the mahogany.

"It's like this," he began.

I appreciated him including me in the conference. He might be a murderer, but it's still nice when someone considers your feelings.

"I heard a lot more than Chester's dying words last night," he said.

"Did you now?" Fleet replied. "What did you hear?"

Nate leaned in:

"I heard it all. Everything Callas said to his killer. I recorded it," he whispered.

18 — Haunting Strain

Fleet gazed back in wonder: not exactly wide eyed, more like through half-closed eyelids. His beard arched slightly, and so did his left eyebrow. I had seen Pixie tilt her head in just such a fashion in her more inquisitive moods.

"You recorded it?"

"I recorded it."

"How?"

Now that he wasn't being accused of anything, Nate was happy to elucidate:

"My hearing aid runs through an app on my phone. Everything I hear, the app hears. If I want to record, all I have to do is tap here. Or perhaps here. Here? All I have to do is tap here," said Nate, tapping. "Comes in handy when I nod off during board meetings."

"And last night you tapped?"

"I tapped," said the good dean. "I was getting some sort of feedback during your speech and had to adjust the setting. After I did, I realized I was picking up on a conversation above us. I looked up and saw Chester Callas talking in one of the fifth-story alcoves."

"Was anyone with him?"

"No. It sounded like he was on the phone. I could only hear his half of the conversation."

"And you decided to record it?"

"I wanted to hear what he was saying," said Nate. "But I also wanted to hear your speech, so I recorded him and listened to you live."

Fleet was honored. "Why didn't you mention this to the police?"

Nate's smile drooped. "I guess I didn't want to shine a light on myself. Some might view my history with Callas as a motive for his death."

"Your history with Callas *was* a motive for his death, Nate."

"Also, I don't like the public knowing I use a hearing aid," continued the dean, listening selectively. "The head of a music college who can barely hear, it's embarrassing."

Fleet didn't know about that. "The hearing aid fits the venue perfectly," he argued. "With it in place, you're your own walking recording studio. So let's hear your greatest hit."

"How's that?"

"The recording, Nate. Chester Callas."

"Oh yes. Yes, of course. The recording," said Nate agreeably. "Now let's see. I believe I tap here...No wait...Maybe here."

Nate tapped there, and with that tap, the ghost of Chester Callas came on line. The recording was kind of staticky, as I believe ghost transmissions frequently are. It started out with a stretch of muffled rustling, then Fleet's speech in the background, and lastly, the faint muttering of Nate saying something about tapping here; no, wait... here; oh that's right, he'd already tapped.

Chester Callas came through clearly:

"...Where are you?...Oh really?...Well, when do we get to meet?...This is silly. You haven't even told me...What's that?...What? You did what!...You psychotic b— [cough] *...But why? What did I—?...When?...But—* [cough] *...Oh yeah? We'll see about that!...* [clunk]*"*

"I dropped the cell there," explained the dean. "And kicked it. It shut off the app."

Fleet asked if that was all of it.

"That was all of it," said Nate. "A few seconds later Callas plummeted to his death."

I noticed Fleet didn't correct him on that point. Chester Callas did plummet, and he was dead, but the plummet hadn't killed him. Not directly.

"Can you give Johnny that audio file, Nate?"

"Of course."

"I'm guessing you can email it?"

"Absolutely. All I have to do is tap," he replied.

"...Where are you?...Oh really?...Well, when do we get to meet?..."

We were sitting huddled around a table in one of the closed-off rooms in the library. Ate and Lesley had joined us, as had Hutton. He was looking peeved that we had excluded him from the interview with Nate Goody. You don't exclude the special consultant to the police.

Fleet was playing the file on my iPhone. He backed up and played the opening lines:

"...Where are you?...Oh really?...Well, when do we get to meet?..."

He hit pause. "I think the other party probably said that they were here, at the banquet. Chester wanted to know why they couldn't meet in person."

"...This is silly. You haven't even told me..."

"You haven't even told me your name," Fleet suggested.

"...What's that?...What? You did what!...You psychotic b— [cough] ..."

"I'll try to fill in the killer's lines now," said the aging DJ. He hit play again, timing his remarks with the pauses.

"What's that?" asked Chet from beyond the grave.

" 'I've just poisoned your champagne.' "

"What? You did what!"

" 'Poisoned you. I slipped it in your drink while you were speaking with your friends. No one saw me.' "

"You psychotic b— [cough]*"*

" 'It's well that you call me that, after what you've done.' "

"But why? What did I—?"

" 'You know what you did.' Obviously we don't know what that is yet," explained Fleet, stepping out of character.

"When?" asked Chester Callas.

" 'You know when,' " Fleet interpreted.

"But— [cough] ..."

" 'It's a fast-acting poison and nearly undetectable. It will appear that you wandered off from the party and succumbed to an allergic reaction.' "

"Oh yeah? We'll see about that! … [clunk]*"*

"Dropping and kicking of Nate's cell phone," I filled in.

Lesley spoke up first. "Do you think he was speaking to a man or a woman?"

"Difficult to say," Fleet replied.

"My guess is a woman," said Hutton. "Sounded like he started to say 'you psychotic bitch' there in line three. No offense," he remarked, bowing to the ladies.

Lesley affected not to mind. "It could have been 'bastard,' " she said. "As in, 'you psychotic bastard,' " she illustrated, staring back at him prettily.

"If you wish to take it that way."

"Yes, yes, but who stabbed him?" I asked. "Assuming the killer operated by remote control, how could he or she have stabbed him over the phone?"

"They didn't," Fleet answered.

"He wasn't stabbed?"

"Not by his killer. Not by anyone. Chester Callas stabbed himself."

"What?" I could understand Chester's self-loathing, but why do it then?

As usual, Fleet had the solution. "Listen to that last line. 'We'll see about that.' The whole conversation Chester is wary, distrustful. He clearly didn't like meeting his mystery party this way. Then it's revealed that he's been poisoned, and the tone changes. His 'We'll see about that' is defiant. He decides to jab himself superficially in the shoulder with his pocket knife. Prompted with that, the police will have to look on his death as suspicious."

"And then he flung himself over the railing?"

"I think we might look on that as a slip. Fortunately, it allowed him to gasp out his last words. Not so fortunate, was his mind had become so addled by the poison that he could only impart a single, cryptic clue. *Frank Sinatra.*"

"Why do you think the killer and he met this way? Over a library phone?"

"That's an interesting question. For one, the library phone couldn't be traced."

That was true. "And I guess the killer wished to keep his or her identity a secret."

"An excellent point, Johnny. Up until the last few moments, Chester seemed unaware that he and the caller had a past. As to what that past consisted of, we can only guess."

I had some thoughts on that.

Fleet read my mind. "There is plenty of history here, especially with two employees of the Pendleton Institute."

"Nate and Victoria," I explained to the uninitiated. "Nate we all know about, but Chet also once blackmailed Victoria over a record deal."

"I think there's more to her motive than simple blackmail," Fleet theorized. "I believe Victoria and Nate's motives interrelate."

I shot an inquisitive stare at Hutton, Lesley and Ate, only to have it returned in triplicate.

"What do you mean?" I asked.

"I mean it was Victoria who first put Chester onto Nate's violin. When Victoria attempted to bribe Chester to help solidify her record deal, she didn't do it with money. She didn't have any. The only bargaining chip she had was Nate Goody's violin, which she had learned about a few days before."

Hutton looked fogged by all this. "So who struck whom with a violin?" he wondered.

"No one," Ate replied. "It was some sort of switcheroo. Victoria switched Nate's violin, and Nate—how many violins were there?"

"I seem to count about six," interjected Lesley. "Is that why Chester fell? Someone hit him with a violin?"

Fleet held up a hand, the maestro calling the orchestra to order. "No one hit anyone with a violin," he said, "least of all Chester Callas." We all nodded. It was one of the few things that hadn't been done to the poor sap. "A few years ago, Victoria had a record deal in the works. It hinged on the word of Chester Callas. She offered to bribe him, not with money, which she didn't have, but, I think, with information. Her old professor, Nate Goody, had inherited a violin and had no inkling of its value. This was what she told Chester. He affected to scorn her bribe—her record deal was already secure—but by then Victoria had said too much. Unlike money, knowledge cannot be refunded. Chester approached Nate, and, as Johnny astutely pointed out earlier, bought the violin for a song, only to turn around and sell the instrument for a fortune. All thanks to Victoria. That was why she was brooding over the old auction brochure last night when I came in. I didn't see what it was, and she tried to hide it under her desk, but I could see it was something she was embarrassed about. Fiddling with Nate's inheritance for her own gain is pretty embarrassing."

Hutton nodded. "You might even say she was instrumental in the instrument's downfall," he said. He frowned. "What? I thought we were doing wordplay."

Fleet continued, "Victoria has managed to keep her role in the transaction a secret all these years. The arrival of Chester this weekend would have placed her in an awkward position."

I was with him. "If Nate ever discovered that she was the one who ratted out the violin, her career here would be over."

"Something to that effect, yes. Nate might seem ineffectual and dithering, but he is also a proud man. He values loyalty above all else. All of which gave Victoria a pretty strong motive for murder, without lessoning Nate's own motive. That's what I meant by interrelated."

There was a short pause, after which Ate said, "I told you it was a switcheroo." She peered between us. For the last five minutes, I had picked up on a certain jumpiness in her manner, as though what we were saying was all well and good, but if we really wanted to hear something cool, all we had to do was shut up and listen. "Can I say my bit now?"

Fleet yielded the floor. Or at least the tabletop. "We're all yours."

"Thanks." She took a deep breath. "Analyzing motives is swell—if you like that sort of thing—but if I've learned anything studying at the foot of the master, it's that everyone has a motive and you can run yourself ragged trying to nail down the winner."

Her argument was sound. When I got framed for murder a few months back—long story—I became well acquainted with this principal. Motives are a dime a dozen, with special deals for price-club members on weekends.

"What we should really be looking at," said Ate, "is the clue."

I smiled. After all the razzing she had endured from Chester Callas, the clue would be the one thing to strike a chord with her.

"We've all submitted our likely candidates, but I have one that beats them all."

We waited patiently for her to let us have it.

She played it coy, just like her dad. "Did anyone else notice the photo of Tanya Saxon in the dean's office?"

We had all noticed it, yes. It was difficult not to notice it.

"Well, I don't know if anyone realized it, but the reason why Tanya was looking like a pinup girl for the Daughters of the American Revolution is, in the photo, she had recently been crowned Miss Hoboken. *Hoboken,*" Ate repeated and smiled expectantly.

I don't know what response she envisioned receiving: cheers perhaps; possibly a sash and tiara crowning her Miss Pendleton Library. Instead, we all stared blankly. The alcove was getting a lot of that that afternoon.

"Don't you get it! *Hoboken.* Sinatra's birthplace? The post office there is named 'Frank Sinatra' for goodness sakes!" She seemed singularly well informed on Hoboken.

"So you think that's what Chester meant when he said Sinatra?" Hutton asked.

"I do."

He nodded. "Why?"

I had to agree. There had to be dozens of people born in Hoboken. Hundreds.

Fleet hated to disappoint her as well, but Hutton was right to be skeptical. "Hoboken holds significance for other suspects as well, my dear. Perhaps you noticed in that same photo, Nate and Lyle were also pictured."

Ate said she hadn't noticed this, no. She was too busy taking in Tanya's ample bosom. Who knew she had one?

"Nevertheless, they were there, albeit not as glamorously. Nate Goody and Lyle Pendleton were also born in Hoboken," said Fleet.

His offspring was a plucky fighter and didn't give up easily. "Yes, well, none of them were crowned Miss Hoboken, were they? And there's something else," she told us. "You know that picture of Tanya—"

We nodded. I believe it was well established that we knew the picture of Tanya.

"Did she look like anyone to you?"

I couldn't say offhand that Tanya did, but it didn't matter, because Ate didn't wait for our answer. "She looked exactly like Ava Gardner," she said.

Again, there was a sense of letdown. "Ava Gardner, the old-time actress?" I asked.

Ate said yes. Was there some other Ava Gardner she didn't know about?

"And this is significant because—"

"Ava Gardner was Sinatra's second wife," said Lesley. Leave it to women to know who was married to whom and in what order.

Ate thanked her. "Maybe you see the significance now?"

Nobody did.

She repeated the question, and her father did his best to study the grain in the tabletop. Hutton said something about a draft coming from the AC vent behind his head, and Lesley attended to a chipped fingernail. I guess it was my turn to employ the friendly raspberry.

"I don't see it. Just because Tanya may or may not have looked a little like Ava Gardner in her youth—"

"She didn't *maybe* look a little like Ava Gardner," said Ate. "She *did* look like her. A lot like her."

"—I still don't see how that links with Chet's clue. If you have the chance to say one last thing on this earth, the one thing that might help finger your murderer, are you going to waste it mentioning the name of somebody who was married to someone who rather resembled the killer in her youth? And how would Chet have known what Tanya looked like in her youth anyway? And if he did know, and he couldn't remember Tanya's name, why not just say Ava Gardner?"

Ate didn't appear to think much of my reasoning, and her sneer showed it. I might not understand much about women, but I know their sneers.

She heaved another sigh. "I thought we had all agreed that Chester's brains were addled. When your brain is addled, you're likely to make all sorts of bizarre associations."

Lesley nodded and smiled in agreement—girl power. Hutton weighed the suggestion but seemed to be coming up short a couple of ounces. Fleet gave her a pat on the shoulder.

I didn't say or do anything.

The one thing that did amaze me, however, was how everyone kept turning up looking like some celebrity in this joint. Ava Gardner. Frank Sinatra (both young and old). Billie Holiday. It was getting out of hand.

"Well, that's me saying my bit," Ate sniffed. "I think you all suck." She looked just like Salma Hayek when she said it.

I leaned back in my chair, nearly sliding down its smooth, hard surface.

"At least we can put one mystery to bed," I said, trying to change the subject and keep the mood light. Any more bickering and we might get a visit from my friend, the shushing librarian. "Now we know why Chester didn't bring his violin with him to the banquet." We did know that, right?

Fleet agreed that we did. "And we know something else as well," he said: "Lyle Pendleton was correct."

I accepted the challenge. "Correct?"

"About the Pendleton Institute. He said something wasn't right about it. That's why he asked me here to investigate."

This was new. "He asked you here to investigate? I thought you were here getting honored as George Enescu's favorite nephew?"

"That was how it was meant to look. The ruse was Lyle's idea. He did enjoy his ruses, that man."

I was probably more amazed by this admission than any of the others. Who knew that old sour face had such a mischievous side?

"It was important that I arrived without anyone suspecting the real reason for the visit."

It seemed to me there were a couple thousand better ways to arrive without anyone suspecting the real reason for your visit, but that was just my opinion. "Should we talk about Lyle's murder now?" I asked.

"No," Fleet replied. "Now we find Pixie." He stood, glancing out the window. "I don't know if that girl took her on a walking tour of the Canary Islands or just the long way around the campus, but I think my dog has had enough exercise for one afternoon."

"I'll find her," said Hutton, standing himself and grimacing from sitting too long. "You want to come?" he asked Ate.

Ate said fine, why not? We were all a bunch of bastards—what difference did it make which one she tagged along with.

"While you're out and about," Fleet offered, "perhaps you could look up Mr. Pratt. I was very interested to learn about Nate's relationship with the burly bandleader. He might have been the one who searched Lyle's office."

"And killed him?" I said, aghast. Not our Henry! "What could he have been searching for?"

"The missing rhapsody, of course."

"But Nate said that was a hoax."

"Perhaps, but too many people have mentioned it for there to be nothing there. Nate, Lyle and Henry Pratt all knew about it—or thought they did. Nate used it to bring Chester Callas here, and so, it would seem from the phone conversation, did the killer. Was the rhapsody merely a lure, or was there more to it than that? We need to consult an expert. Since everyone appears to be pairing off, perhaps you would like to join me in that endeavor, Johnny?"

I said I supposed I would, showing about as much enthusiasm as his daughter had for Hutton's offer. It wouldn't have been my first choice, consulting with some dry old expert, but what else did I have to do?

I had a feeling we were leaving someone out. I looked back at the table and smiled. Lesley. My fiancée!

"Do you want to come too?" I asked her.

I realized this wouldn't technically be pairing off, but when Enescu Fleet's one of the pair I seldom had anything meaningful to lend to the conversation anyway.

Lesley said she'd have to catch up with us later. "I told a gal I'd meet with her about our wedding reception. You know, Johnny, you could join me on that."

I agreed that I could—but darn it all, I had already told Fleet that I would help him out with his expert. I was all keyed up for it.

"It's fine," she said. "You know, I wonder if Sergei Brodovitch would agree to play at the wedding. I know it's not the typical thing, having a classical pianist perform, but when you look like he does, who cares?"

So we were on that again, were we? I knew what this was. It was the bad-boy syndrome. It seemed to run in the family with the Darlingtons. Lesley's father, I recently learned, had been quite the rascal in his youth, and about a month ago her sister, Jill, had started dating the son of a prominent New England hoodlum—nice guy; I liked him.

As far as I was concerned, Lesley could have her little infatuation. As long as she kept Sergei behind the piano and not under it, what did I care? I was the man she loved, not him.

I left the library telling myself that.

19 — The Virtuoso Touch

As Fleet and I crossed to one of the smaller venue concert halls, he explained that our investigation needed its own change of venue. "We've had lots of Sinatra," he said. "It's about time we viewed this case from a more classical angle."

"More classic than Sinatra?" I wouldn't have thought that possible.

He whisked open the door and headed inside. "Come, Johnny, we're late."

I didn't see how one could be late if one had no clue where one was going, but the elegance of my argument was obscured by the fact that he wasn't listening. I had barely dodged the heavy door he had not bothered to hold open, when I looked up and saw him shoot across the musty lobby, a blur of khaki slacks and vented tweed. I picked up my feet and followed him down some stairs and through another weighty door, this time narrowly managing to avoid it slamming in my face.

We were in a darkened auditorium: heavy mahogany walls with a smattering of art. It was an intimate setting, two banks of folding chairs of roughly eighty seats each, all occupied.

I should say nearly all occupied. We located two in the back just as the applause started. I didn't think it was for us—although Fleet did tend to get a nice hand many places he went.

"What is all this?" I asked.

"Our expert is about to perform," he replied. Then he shushed me.

I frowned. If I wanted to be shushed, I would have stayed in the library. The clapping eased up, and the hall went silent, short of a couple sniffs and coughs. You always have a few of the nasal brigade at these performances.

A man with an especially knobby head blocked my view initially, but a bit of shifting and I was able to peek through to the focal point of the room.

I was pleasantly surprised. When Fleet said an expert, I had pictured some woolly old professor with pince-nez and a bow tie: a cross between Nate Goody and Lyle Pendleton, without the former's sharp mind and the latter's personality. When Fleet told me this expert would be performing, I upgraded my expectations to a woolly old professor with pince-nez and a striped bow tie. Maybe even paisley.

What we got was Rachel Barton Pine.

Far from the dry old expert I had been envisioning, RBP was a splendent young virtuoso with long red hair, a bright smile and large, luminous eyes. She wore an ecru-colored gown and was holding the instrument of the hour, a violin. I wondered if it was a Guarneri. I remembered Tanya Saxon mentioning Rachel Pine earlier, in re the concerts this weekend, and now we had her.

There were a couple preliminaries first; then the presenter made himself scarce. Rachel was on. She lifted her bow and began to play like a house on fire. I got winded just watching her.

I wouldn't have recognized the piece offhand, but after the first few passages she took a moment to give us the skinny on the compositions: a sort of running commentary, which I gathered was something of her trademark.

The pieces were Paganini, just like the "Theme of" Sergei Brodovitch had played for the girls and me a few hours ago: the little ditty that would forever have my fiancée kicking herself for accepting offers of marriage before entertaining all possible candidates.

I thought Rachel was better, and I'm not just saying that because I wished to see Sergei bludgeoned to death by a trombone. She was damn good. And informative too—especially helpful to a layman like myself, who wouldn't know a fortissimo from whatever the opposite of a fortissimo is. I learned a lot about Paganini in the next hour, much of which I've now forgotten, but I was left with a solid impression of his virtuosity and showmanship. Apparently he was of a dour temperament as well, as evidenced by the portrait of the bloke hanging on the back wall. It was painted by another bloke called Delacroix, who also appeared to take a dark view of life.

The concert wrapped up in time for lunch, which was good because I was starving.

I came out from washing up to find the virtuoso had joined Fleet at our table. Not Paganini, which would have been awkward, but Rachel Barton Pine.

I slid in across from her, and Fleet made the introductions.

"We were just talking about old times," he said, and I replied with a slight nod and what I could almost guarantee was a fairly chowderheaded smile.

I'm never at my best around celebrities, and when these celebrities start reminiscing about old times with Enescu Fleet, I'm truly out of my depth.

I never know what to say. Should I inquire about these old times? Act like I know all about them? Order a sandwich? It's a poser. When you've lived the life of danger Enescu Fleet has, how's a mere mortal like myself going to keep up?

"Old times, eh?" I said, wishing I had left it at the chowderheaded smile.

"Those were some adventures we had," declared Rachel Barton Pine. "So much intrigue."

Fleet said indeed. "Lisbon in '98…"

"And Singapore…"

"And let's not forget Prague," concluded the dashing PI, smiling himself now.

My own smile did not falter. It remained glued to my face—my silly, clueless face.

I got it; they were doing geography. I liked geography. That didn't really help me, though. Short of repeating the list of locales back to them, I had nothing to add to the discussion.

It turned out I wasn't meant to have anything to add. Before I could reply, "Lisbon, eh?" Rachel Barton Pine burst out in laughter. "I think we've had our fun, Ef."

Fleet supposed they had. He turned to me and revealed, "I met Rachel a few years back, through her husband Greg. I looked into a matter on behalf of his consulting firm."

I nodded slowly. "Not in Lisbon?"

"No."

"Not Singapore or Prague?"

"Not this time, no."

I nodded, more forcefully this time. Ate was right. He sucked.

The important thing was, we could now order lunch. Rachel had more violin-ing to do and would dine later. As for Fleet, outside the occasional *amuse-bouche* or cocktail garnish, I couldn't recall ever seeing him eat.

That left me. In deference to my abstemious tablemates, I passed on the double cheeseburger and fries I had been dreaming of and ordered a bowl of soup, crab. (When you're in Maryland, you eat crab. If you ask me, you also eat double cheeseburgers, but I could rough it.)

As it turned out, I had made a good selection. After the initial mirth at my expense, the mood at the table shifted to a more solemn tone, not conducive to fried meat. "I can't believe there's a killer at the Pendleton," said Rachel, and I was struck again by how buoyant she was, even discussing murder. I had heard one of the audience members, a girl of about eight, asking her after the concert if she was a mermaid, and it seemed to me she did look a little like a mermaid—at the moment a mermaid who had swum into choppy seas, but a mermaid who was keeping her red head above the waves and her song pure. "I would have postponed the performance had I known."

Fleet dismissed the notion. "That wouldn't have helped anyone, believe me. We all must play our part in life. Mine is to bring a killer to justice—yours, to make the world a better place with your music."

Rachel frowned. "We should try switching roles sometime. I'll find the killer, and you play the violin. That reminds me. You promised to play the clarinet at one of my performances."

I gazed between Rachel Barton Pine, world-renowned violinist, and Enescu Fleet, world-famous detective and (apparently) clarinetist. This was the first I had heard of any clarinet, but most things about Fleet I picked up along the way.

"Nobody wants that, I'm sure," the man of mystery demurred.

"I don't know," she said. "I would consider it an honor jamming with a real-life descendent of George Enescu."

"You heard about that?"

"I did. You do know you're not a real-life descendent of George Enescu, don't you?"

"Shh!" said Fleet archly, and I was happy I wasn't the only one he shushed. "We're not keeping you from your next gig, are we?" he asked, and Rachel agreed that she did have another performance at three, but she could give us a couple minutes.

"You said I might be able to help you with something?"

"I'm certain you can. How well did you know the murdered man?"

"Lyle Pendleton? Not well. I'm familiar with the family, of course."

"Not Lyle," said Fleet. "Chester Callas."

"Oh, Chester. Yes—I did meet him a couple of times," she replied with a frown—the only way to remember meeting Chester Callas.

"Was he a competent violinist?"

"Competent? I would say competent, yes. More than competent, really. He was solid. Good execution."

Here, I could have said something incredibly witty, asking *Which one, his murder or his playing?* but I didn't know how well this would go over, so I said nothing.

I went back to my soup.

"His technique was sound. It was his understanding of the music that lacked."

"An odd failing to have in a music critic."

"I know. He wasn't a very good one of those either."

"But he was a good technician on the violin?"

"Not just the violin, on many instruments. The technical side came easily to him: the math in the music. The emotion did not. I always felt he liked numbers better than people. His playing had no humanity."

"You wouldn't expect it would," I said. "You have to be human to play with humanity," I quipped (possibly with incredible wit, I can't say).

Rachel nodded gradually, still uncertain what to make of me, and I chomped down on one of those little salted crackers they give you with soup. Love those things.

"I understand he had a good memory?" asked Fleet.

"Eidetic, from what I gather," answered Rachel.

Fleet pondered. "A flair for numbers. Perfect memory…Interesting."

Rachel and I exchanged quizzical looks. Were we meant to partake in this discussion? Now she knew how I felt.

He reached in his pocket and produced the list of phone extensions he had collected. "What do you make of these?"

She looked at the list.

"You mentioned the math in music," he said. "Anything *musical* in these numbers?"

"Nothing I can see. They don't correspond to any scale or arrangement. Sorry."

Fleet wasn't concerned. "Don't be sorry, Rachel. You've already helped out a ton." He stood to leave her to her next performance.

"I don't know about a ton," she replied. "I do have a question of my own."

"Fire away."

"Is it true Chester muttered something about Sammy Davis Jr. when he died?"

"Not Sammy. Frank Sinatra."

"Oh. Well, that makes *a lot* more sense," said Rachel, standing herself now. "You're coming to the second half of the concert, aren't you? The last twelve caprices?"

"We'd be delighted."

"It starts at three. There may be a few more people in the audience with this one. Oh, and you won't want to miss the one tonight." She peered my way. "You're all invited."

I thanked her and told her that my fiancée and I would be thrilled to attend. That is, if the killer hasn't gutted me with a piccolo or something before then. I would pencil her in.

The site of the second half of Rachel's concert was the Rondo Auditorium. Fleet and I spent the walk there reviewing the finer points from lunch.

Considering that we had had an expert on hand, all ready to *expertize* her heart out, we hadn't asked a lot of the questions I would have.

He made no mention of the missing Romanian Rhapsody—was there one or wasn't there?—nor did he bring up Nate's violin. Apparently Fleet required no additional advice on these matters and had asked everything he needed to ask.

I wasn't so certain about that.

It seemed to me he had hoped for more on the phone extensions. I think he thought there was some kind of musicality to the numbers in the list, and to find none had let him down. But he would never show it. That was Ef. You can't sink a Fleet.

We arrived at the Rondo and found what Rachel Pine had called a few more audience members amounted to several thousand more. Evidently the first half of the concert had been invitation only, a select assembly of patrons of the arts, industry folk and retired private detectives who may or may not secretly play the clarinet. The second half the Pendleton Institute had opened up to the world. From the looks of it, a good deal of the world had accepted the offer.

We took our place in the queue as the gathering throng closed in around us.

"Nice turnout," said Fleet.

I grunted a yes. I preferred being one of the special people.

After a few minutes, I turned to check our place in line and nearly swallowed my chewing gum—which was weird, because I had spit out my chewing gum ten minutes ago.

"Something up, Johnny?"

Up? He could bet his khaki ass there was something up! "Look," I said.

He looked. About twenty yards back, nestled in among the various free-concert goers, was the Romanian.

20 — Trailing Melody

"Looks like your friend will be joining us in the festivities," Fleet remarked.

He was no friend of mine. "Should I call the police?" I whispered—don't know why, there was no way he could have heard us from that distance. Nate perhaps, but not the Romanian.

Fleet vetoed the move. "He will only run off as soon as the authorities show their faces. I have a better idea."

"Yes?"

"He's clearly here for you. You lead him off down the alley, and I'll follow and see what he does to you."

"Yes?" I said, still waiting for that better idea.

"Don't worry. I can see from here he's not packing a trombone."

I don't know why people listen to Enescu Fleet. Because his name's Enescu? That must be it. You listen to the composer George Enescu; why not listen to the detective Enescu Fleet? The way I was feeling then, I would have just as soon given them both a miss.

The last thing he said to me—the detective, not the composer—was "Don't look back." This was fine advice in theory, but it didn't hold up in practice. As I strolled away from the crowd and moseyed oh so casually down the path toward the alley, my only desire—the only thing I ever wanted in this world, it felt like—was to look back. Just a peek, a glimpse over my shoulder. Anything. That was all I asked.

I made it all the way into the shade of the Rondo, and maybe twenty yards down the line of the thin little imitation sidewalk they like to put in alleyways, before I cracked. I twirled around and looked back with all my might.

There was nobody there. Whether something or someone had spooked him, or the thin little sidewalk had proven too much for him to bear, I couldn't say, but he had vanished. Maybe he hadn't followed me, after all. Either way, he was Fleet's to deal with now. I took a breath and rotated slowly back to the fore, only to bound back in horror.

He was here!

I gulped a couple times and looked closer and saw that, in fact, he wasn't. Hutton was, which wasn't nearly as bad.

Ate was with him. "Heya, Hathaway."

"Heya, Ate."

"You don't look so good, Hathaway."

"I don't feel so good, Ate."

Now that we had worked that out, I gave Hutton the once-over, and found that he didn't look so good either. (Ate looked fine.) "Did you catch up with Henry Pratt?"

Ate rolled her eyes. Hutton took off his specs and gave them a polish, so I wouldn't miss him rolling his as well. "Pratt has done a bunk," he said.

"He's done a what?"

"A bunk."

"He's vamoosed," Ate clarified. Finally, someone speaking English.

"You mean he's lammed it?" I asked.

"Like a Greek gyro," Hutton replied, peering back at Ate. She filled in:

"We caught up with the band in one of the practice rooms beneath Adagio Hall. Band! More like gang. The worst set of thugs and cutthroats you'd ever want to meet."

"Think Hell's Angels with tassels," said Hutton.

"Apparently at the Pendleton, all the tough kids join the band," she explained.

I nodded. Sort of a switch, that. "And they told you Henry Pratt vamoosed?"

"What we could make out from their grunts and growls, yes."

"—talking out of the sides of theirs mouths and toying with their flick-knives all the while," added Hutton.

"Actually rinsing out their mouthpieces," she corrected. "But they rinsed with menace."

"And what exactly did they say?" I wondered.

"They said Pratt ditched them before they left for the competition in Scranton, causing them to wash out in the first round. They were pretty ticked about it. No one has seen him since."

I took this information on board. "Pratt was leaving for his competition when he and I bumped into each other in this very alley. That was right after Lyle Pendleton was killed."

"I think Pratt did it. He and Lyle Pendleton were privy to the discovery of the missing Romanian Rhapsody. I bet Pratt went to the villa looking for the score, Lyle startled him in his search, and he killed him. Pratt killed Lyle," she said.

Yeah, I got that. Something didn't seem right, though. "But the score was a fake. What they thought they found they hadn't found at all."

"Well, maybe one of them knew that what they thought they hadn't found they had found, after all," she argued.

I blinked at her. "What?"

"I think Pratt's the killer."

I said fine. What did I care? "But what about Chester Callas?"

"What about him?"

"Didn't the band alibi him for the Callas murder?"

"With a menace," she agreed.

"Well then. Are we looking for two murderers or one?"

She didn't know. She couldn't speak to the Callas murder, she could only speak to the Lyle one. For that, Henry had motive, opportunity and—"What's the third thing?"

"I don't think there is one."

"I'm certain there is. Motive, opportunity—darn, almost had it. You don't know?"

I didn't. Maybe it was missing, like the Third Romanian Rhapsody.

I turned to Hutton. Did he know?

Hutton didn't know. Hutton didn't appear to know anything. "What?" he asked. He didn't seem right either.

Ate concurred. "What's with you anyway? You've been acting wonky ever since you came out of your room at the Adagio."

So something about our dorm room had upset him, had it? It couldn't have been the decor—he would have noticed that last night.

"Feel like hearing some caprices?" I offered. "I'll tell you right off, though, you've skipped the first twelve, so you might not be able to follow the plot."

Like Nate Goody, Hutton came clean. He had something to reveal to us. "You know the girl who offered to walk Pixie while we were in with Nate Goody?"

I knew the girl who offered to walk Pixie. Not personally. But I could pick her out of a lineup.

"Well, after we all split up outside the library, we went looking for her. Ate and I did."

I remembered this too. Fleet had asked them to look. "And?"

"We couldn't find her. The girl. Ate suggested we check in on Henry Pratt and his goons instead, and that's what we did."

I nodded. We were all up to speed. "This is pretty fascinating, Hutton…"

"I didn't think about the dog again," he proceeded, "until after we met with the band. We talked, and then I went upstairs to our room for a minute, and there was this letter."

"A letter?" asked Ate. This was the first she had heard of any letters.

"A note," said Hutton. "Sort of a communiqué, if you want to call it that…"

"What did it say!" we demanded.

Hutton frowned. "I have it here somewhere," he said, feeling around in his pockets. He shook his head. "I'll give you the gist. The girl—the one who offered to walk Pixie—she has also done a vamoose. The letter spelled it out: the Maltese has been dognapped."

21 — Conspicuous Silence

The words didn't immediately register. I can't figure why. They were so straightforward.

"Someone snatched the dog?"

"That's what I said, isn't it?"

"But why?" squeaked Ate.

"The letter did not specify."

She asked him what it did specify, and he replied not a whole hell of a lot. "The writer wanted us to know that Pixie was safe and would be presented to her owner in due course."

"Providing what?"

"It did not specify."

I muttered something under my breath. I didn't know about Ate, but I was getting fed up with this letter writer's lack of specifics. "Who sent it? Wait, let me guess: it didn't specify?"

Hutton agreed that it didn't, no. "It was handwritten, if that's helpful."

It wasn't. "Could you identify the handwriting?"

"Of course not."

"Did it look, well—Romanian?"

He glared. "How the hell should I know?"

"You have a Romanian name, don't you?"

"Yes, but that doesn't make me an expert on the country's penmanship. I'm British. What do I know about Romania? They like their *tzatziki* sauce—that's about it."

"That's Greece," said Ate. Unlike Hutton, she did know something about her name's country of origin—even if she wasn't any more Greek than Hutton was Romanian. "Greek cuisine is the one that uses a tzatziki. It's a yogurt sauce."

He conceded the fact. "I guess I still have gyros on the brain. Anyone else hungry? We haven't lunched yet."

This was no time for talking about food. I had to make do with soup and crackers; he didn't see me carping about it. "Never mind lunch," I said. "The murderer has just become a dognapper."

"You think the killer is behind it?"

Why wouldn't I? "Who else would want to snatch Pixie? The ankle bites alone would be enough to dissuade all but the most desperate. With her in hand, the killer calls the shots."

"So Pixie has become a cat's-paw, then?"

"Something like that," I remarked, assuming he didn't mind mixing his metaphors. "We have to find her before the killer assembles the ultimate mousetrap."

"Oh, so there's mice now too, is there?"

There were always mice, I said. We were the mice. "Unless we act. We have to find Pixie before the killer makes us so. Mice," I qualified. "Instead of men. And women," I added.

"It's beginning to sound like a regular menagerie," grumbled Hutton. "So where do we begin?" he asked Ate. I don't know why he was asking her. I was there too.

She didn't know, but however we did this, we had to do it without her dad finding out. "He's got enough on his mind without hearing how we lost his dog. You have no idea what that mutt means to him. She was Mom's, the last thing he ever gave to her. I sometimes think he cares more about—it's not important. We have to find her."

That's what I said. "What about the girl?" I asked. "The intern who spirited Pixie away?"

Hutton didn't think much of the lead. "She was simply an agent of the dognapper. We won't get anywhere with her. She probably wasn't even a real intern."

Ate wasn't so quick to gloss over the femme fatale angle. "She has to have some connection with the culprit. You don't remember anything about her?"

"Like what?"

"I don't know. Some clue to her identity?"

"Such as a variance in her diphthong, indicating that she had recently spent some time in the coastal villages of Nova Scotia? No, sorry. She was just an everyday, cute librarian chick."

"Oh, so she was cute now, was she?"

"Rather cute, yes."

"I didn't think she was all that cute."

"You saw her?"

"From a distance."

"And you feel you can determine cuteness from a distance?"

"In so far as cuteness can be quantified—yes, I do. If you want to know what I think, I think she looked like a dog-swiping, painted-up harlot."

"From a distance?"

"From a distance, yes."

"Well, I didn't hear anyone saying anything about painted-up harlots when we were handing Pixie over. Perhaps you could have voiced some of those concerns then, and we wouldn't be in this mess."

"So it's my fault now, is it?"

"Fault is a strong word."

"You know what else is a strong word..." she said.

"*People, people,*" I yelled. That's the one nice thing about an alley, you can yell all you want and nobody cares. "This is no time for quibbling over cuteness. A Maltese's life is at stake. Let's just agree that the girl who swiped Pixie was a cute and luscious treat and leave it at that."

"Luscious?" asked Ate.

"I'm not sure I'd call her luscious," said Hutton.

"Does Lesley know you call other girls luscious?" wondered Ate.

I was getting a headache. I turned to Hutton. "Do you have the letter or don't you?"

He did. He pulled it out from his pocket and handed it over.

He was right: there wasn't much to go on:

Mr. Enescu,

We will PRESENT your dog to you in due COURSE—unless you locate us first, that is. Until then, she is safe.

The Grand Proctor

If I had to guess, the handwriting did look pretty Romanian.

"What's it written on?" asked Ate. She tugged at the sheet. "Why's it all glossy?"

I had noticed that too. "It looks like the killer tore the page out from a magazine."

"Course catalog," corrected Hutton.

He was right again. On the back of the paper was a list of Pendleton classes. Clearly the killer/dognapper believed in recycling. "Why are *present* and *course* in caps?" I asked.

"Oo, oo, I think I got it!" gasped Ate, bouncing around the alley.

"Got what?" said Hutton.

"Where they're keeping Pixie. It's a code!"

"Code?"

"Look at the course numbers on the back. They put them on the doors here. I noticed it earlier when Lesley and I were out exploring. It stood out in my mind, because when I was in school the course numbers never had anything to do with the room numbers. I used to spend the first month of every semester finding my classes."

I did too. Frequently I would just give up and go shoot billiards.

Ate continued, "I guess the school here is small enough that they don't have to shift the courses around; each one can stay in one place; one classroom to a course."

I was with her on the course numbers, and her thoughts on the size of the college were well reasoned and sound. But what did this have to do with finding Pixie?

"Don't you get it? Read the letter: it's taunting us. *The Grand Proctor. Unless you can locate us first.* It's a test. The people who have Dad's dog want us to find them. They will *present* her to him in *due course*. Course. Present. When do you get presents? Your birthday. Look at it—the page on the back has an ad for the banquet last night. Now look at the list. Most of the course numbers could correspond to a date. 428: April 28th. 525: May 25th. And on and on. Get it?"

I got it. As Henry Pratt would say, I dug her. "All we have to do, then, is match up your dad's birthday to a room number, and that will lead us to his dog?"

Ate sighed. It was so difficult interacting with morons, she was thinking. "No, you dolt, not my dad's birthday—how would the culprit know my dad's birthday? I don't even know my dad's birthday. The letter is addressed to *Mr. Enescu,* not Mr. Fleet. The clue is George Enescu's birthday—yesterday, the night of the banquet. August 19th."

I said aha. That did make more sense. And I did recall Nate Goody mentioning that yesterday was George Enescu's birthday.

I knew there had to be a Romanian angle.

"Come on," said Ate, bolting down the alleyway—not using the sidewalk, I noticed, but she was excited. "I think I saw a campus directory earlier. Room 819, here we come!"

After consulting the directory, we learned that Room 819 was in the Cabriole Building on the outskirts of the campus. The halls were mostly deserted now, the doors locked.

Fortunately we thought to bring Hutton, and Hutton his lock-picking kit. He had 819 open in a matter of seconds. Now all that remained was the subtle turning of the knob and the quick burst across the threshold.

"Ready?" asked Ate.

"Ready?" asked Hutton.

"Ready," replied I.

I would have felt more ready if I knew what it was we were bursting in on. Hopefully the element of surprise would supersede any strategic advantage the dognapper(s) had.

"On three," she said.

"Three," said Hutton.

"Three," I agreed. *Three* for the missing rhapsody and the three working brain cells of Pixie the dog. *Viva Romania and Malta!*

One. Two. Three. In we burst.

After that buildup, you had to figure there would be nobody inside to see it. There wasn't. The overhead lamps were off, but there was enough light pouring in from the row of windows that we could see that we had crashed a small, stacked lecture hall. There wasn't a single dog, cat's-paw or mousetrap stirring.

"I was certain we had it right," sighed Ate.

Hutton strolled up and down the hardwood at the foot of the tiny amphitheater. His arms were behind his back, his head down in thought: very much the pensive instructor addressing the invisible student body. All he needed was a cap and gown to make the portrait complete.

"It *feels* right," he agreed.

"Maybe Nate Goody misspoke," I said. "Maybe Enescu wasn't born on August 19th. Maybe he was born in December or March. Or maybe the person who kidnapped Pixie didn't think to send us a coded message at all."

Hutton's head jerked up. "Say that again."

"Maybe they didn't send us a coded message—"

"Not that. Of course they sent us a coded message! The other part."

"Maybe he wasn't born on August 19th?"

"Yes!" He went to the chalkboard and began jotting something out. "I might not know tzatziki," he said, "but I know calendars. Romania didn't adopt the Gregorian calendar until 1919."

"What one are we on now?" I asked.

"Gregorian."

"Is this new?"

"No, Hath. Most of the Western world has been on the Gregorian since the 1700s."

And Romania didn't get to it until 1919? Those scamps! Who needed yogurt? They made their own fun.

Hutton continued his calculations. "That means in 1881, when George Enescu was born, August 19 would have actually been—" He scrawled away. "August 7th."

"Room 807!" exclaimed Ate.

They dashed out together, and I was left to switch off the lights and shut the door. Somebody had to do it.

Room 807 proved much more dynamic than 819. It was around the corner and down a long hallway all on its own. But that wasn't the dynamic part.

"I can hear movement inside," said Hutton, placing his head to the door. He reached up and jiggled the knob. "It's unlocked," he whispered.

We had already done the *ready* thing and the *one-two-three.* We could skip all that now.

In we burst (again).

This time the lecture hall was not deserted. In fact, it wasn't a lecture hall at all. It was a dance studio. You know the sort: polished blond wood on the floor, walls of mirrors, those long leg bars that make a normal person's groin ache just looking at them.

In the back corner lay Pixie on a bed of blankets. Her tummy was turned up in the air, and her little paws twitched playfully as she slept. She had a cup of what I could only assume was Fiji by her side. I was sorry she had to be put through this ordeal.

Across from the dog bed stood a studio-style piano, no doubt normally occupied by the dancing instructor. I could picture the teacher sitting there, banging the lid with a walking stick whenever the dancers fell short of the ideal.

A man stood by it now, his back to us. He was leaning over a woman at the keys, the pair speaking in hushed tones. I couldn't see her above the neck, but I took it this was the luscious accomplice. Whoever she was, I felt like we were horning in on something pretty intimate.

As we approached, the man straightened up, revealing himself to be Sergei Brodovitch.

He looked as rugged and handsome as ever, the bastard—the chiseled jaw, that playful gap between his teeth. I was shocked. For all his faults, I never would have taken him for a Pixie-snatcher.

This dramatic unveiling might have held me more spellbound had my attention not been diverted by the woman sitting at the piano. Far from his luscious female operative, she was my luscious female fiancée, Lesley.

22 — Má Vlast

I was shocked once more and appalled.

Lesley—the woman I loved and planned to marry! Lesley—the woman I had already (if I understood what she was telling me earlier) put a deposit down on a reception hall with!

The girl had gone Czech!

The room began to pirouette around my head. I guess I was in the right place for it.

I didn't know what was worse, that we had discovered them cheek to jowl, or that they had made Pixie a party to their guilty liaison. I think it had to be the dog. It somehow made the whole affair that much more crass and unseemly.

Spotting us at last, Lesley bounded up from the piano bench.

"John! What are you doing here?"

I could only shake my head and spout incoherently. Her lovely lips parted in a frown. She could always interpret my incoherent mutters better than most.

"Johnny, this isn't what it looks like!"

I smiled the valiant smile of a man who would never love again. I appreciated that she thought enough of what we once had together to dust off that old evergreen. So much kinder than giving my face a patronizing pat and telling me that I wasn't half the man my rival was.

"I—oh hell, I can't explain now," she huffed.

Taking in the rest of my extraction team in a glance—trying their darnedest to look anywhere but at us—she uttered, "Where's Fleet?"

I smiled another valiant one. I appreciated that she thought enough of what we had to ask where Fleet was, but…Actually I had no clue why she wanted to know where Fleet was. It didn't seem to square with the scene at all.

"What?"

"Sergei thought Enescu Fleet would come himself."

"Is that what Sergei thought?"

"It was. That was the idea. He wanted to be certain that Fleet was the man he, Sergei, thought he was. That he could be trusted. I told him I would vouch for him, for Fleet I mean, and that seemed A-okay with Sergei. I meant to call and explain, but then we got caught up playing the 'Minute Waltz,' and I totally forgot. It's a long story," she remarked, correctly interpreting the baffled look on my face. She was as good at interpreting my confused looks as she was my mutters.

She took a deep breath. "You remember what we were saying earlier today? About Sergei's involvement with the Czech mafia?"

I told her I remembered.

"Well, that wasn't too far off. It's—oh, bollocks!"

"Bollocks?" I wondered.

"Bollocks," said Lesley.

I considered the remark. Bollocks. It was all bollocks, she said. I couldn't speak for Hutton or Ate, but I was satisfied. No further explanation required.

Then I got it. Her pithy interjection had less to do with her narrative, and more to do with a live development in the studio.

I could hear someone breathing behind me. Turning, I saw a large man, a foot taller than Hutton, with a shaved head. I couldn't fathom how he had slipped in, but now that he was here, I recognized the skull. It was the same knobby protrusion I had been forced to look around during the Rachel Barton Pine concert. I wondered how long he had been with us, and which of the first twelve caprices he liked better. I liked number nine.

Evidently my fellow attendee favored a stony glare over actual conversation. Outside the breathing, he didn't make a peep, leaving the speaking to a darkly bearded individual who now joined us from the direction of the dance instructor's office. (I thought for a minute that he could be the dancer instructor, but he didn't have a walking stick, so that couldn't be right.)

He strolled across the polished wood, smiling warmly. He was shadowed by a trio of associates, all shaved up top and stony of brow. I know I've been saying this a lot, but they had a foreign air about them. "Romanians?" I asked Lesley.

"Czechs," she answered.

I nodded. That was my second guess.

As previously indicated, the lead Czech had a beard, not all that thick but expansive. It covered him from cheekbone to Adam's apple. He had head hair too, not much but some; a prominent nose, this sloping downward; and a long, drooping countenance. It was as though someone had taken the face of a normal bearded representative of the Czech Republic and stretched it out with a rolling pin.

His eyes fell on Sergei. "We meet again, *kamarád.*"

The phenom offered no rejoinder to this greeting. Perhaps he didn't know what a *kamarád* was. I was pretty sure it was some kind of melon.

"You did not seriously believe you could hide from your past forever?"

Again, Sergei made no attempt to speak. He shot his cuffs defiantly.

"What the hell is going on here?" I demanded. (I ask this a lot, I know.)

The speaker turned his bearded grin my way, looking straight through me, as most men of stature do.

"This man"—he indicated Sergei Brodovitch—"left my employ some time ago. We are here to bring him back where he belongs."

"No kidding," I replied. "Well, off you go."

Lesley had other ideas. "You can't!" She twirled around and gave us a pleading look. "We can't let them take him!"

Hutton frowned and said, "Um..." while Ate arched an eyebrow and said, "What?"

I had to agree. I didn't know what she expected us to do about it.

"They'll kill him!" said Lesley.

I found this hard to believe. "You wouldn't kill him, would you?"

"Of course not," answered the beard, still not looking at me. He only had eyes for Sergei.

"See," I told Lesley. "Of course they wouldn't."

"I want him to work as my personal pianist," continued the man.

"See," I also continued. "He wants him to work as his personal pianist."

Lesley responded with another of her huffs. "He's being facetious, Johnny!"

I frowned. I didn't much care for facetiousness. "Are you being facetious?" I asked the man.

"Of course not, *kamarád*."

"See, not facetious," I passed along, frowning at the *k* crack. I didn't much care for people who called me melons.

Lesley threw up her hands. I was hopeless. She gave the other dominant male in the room a shot: "Hutton..."

The question appeared to unman him. "What?"

This time Lesley didn't even bother tossing her hands. "Ate?" she asked.

"Um," said the dominant female.

It was about time Sergei got in on the action. He did so in the form of a protest: "I am not the man that you think I am!"

The beard disagreed. "Ah, but you are. Exactly the man I think that you are. A certain South American despot, he did not know the man he thought you were, and now he does. Or rather, he *did*."

I was finding all this a touch trying between the temples. Romanians, Czechs and now certain South American despots. This conversation was becoming a regular melting pot—and not to its advantage, either.

Sergei seemed to concur. "I do not understand what you are speaking of."

The beard sighed. He clearly expected more from his little *kamarád*.

"This has grown tiresome," he announced. He waved a manicured hand in our direction. "Dispose of the bodies of these four," he told his men.

Call me overly sensitive, but it seemed to me this conversation had taken an unpleasant turn in the last few seconds. It all depended how one meant *dispose of bodies.* Did he mean dispose with a meat ax, or was this some quaint Czech colloquialism I was not familiar with?

Hutton was curious about this himself. "You know, not to gum up your plans or anything, but we can dispose of our own bodies."

Ate backed him up: "He's right. There's no reason to go to any trouble."

I also threw my support into the ring. When it comes to bodies, you can't beat self-disposal, I said.

The beard was no longer listening to us—which was too bad because we were never going to master his native expressions without him. One of his men—the heavy breather—leaned in and whispered something in his ear, distracting his attention.

"The dog?" repeated the boss. He gazed down at Pixie, the furball prancing over to see which one of us wished to rub her stomach. The leader frowned. "We will bring the dog with us," he said. "She shall entertain my mistress."

This was a relief. I don't know what I would have done if the man's mistress had been deprived of fresh entertainment.

"Dog, we bring?" clarified the henchman, trying out English for the first time.

"Dog we bring," agreed his employer.

The man nodded, as if to say "Excellent choice, sir"—the suck-up—and bent over to haul the canine in.

I could have told him his approach was all wrong. You don't pick up Pixie, you *finesse* her into your arms. It's like throwing a pass to a receiver on the run. You don't reach for where she *is*; you reach for where she is *going to be* (unless you're Enescu Fleet, whose magnetic personality could win over half the animal kingdom without lifting a finger).

The henchman possessed no such magnetism. He stooped and reached, and Pixie moved. He stooped and reached again, and Pixie shot between his legs and came to rest ten feet away. It might have been amusing had it not been for that body-disposal thing.

She was panting alongside another of the Czechs now, a serious-minded individual who preferred not to get involved.

The hunter became a man of iron; a dogcatcher the Czech Republic could look on with pride. He froze, breathing steadily through his nostrils (still noisily). All around him, his furry quarry bounded and pranced, taunting him. But he paid her no mind. He was waiting for his chance…

He sprang. He still missed, but he showed much better form. He came up smiling. He was close, very close. He bent over again, and that's when Sergei Brodovitch made his move.

The couple of times I had seen the phenom noodling away at the keyboard, I hadn't appreciated how fast his hands were. There was no doubt about their speed now.

As the stooping nimrod tiptoed past, Sergei darted forward and pulled the man's blazer up and over his head, turning it into a pin-striped straightjacket. From there, he kneed the oaf in the face, spun and jammed an elbow into the astonished gape of a second combatant coming to his colleague's aid. For his encore, he snatched the latter's pistol from its holster and stunned another assailant with a quick blow to the nose with the stock.

Only one henchman remained, and Hutton and the ladies attended to him. Hutton stepped back and stomped him on the foot; Ate gave him a sharp boot in the gonads; and Lesley gave him another sharp one, also in the gonads. Then Hutton grabbed his gun. If I hadn't known better, I'd have said they had been practicing these moves for weeks.

I suppose during all this I might have done something myself, got in on the act somehow, but I had not been practicing the moves for weeks, or even days. The steps were all new to me. What you needed was an understudy.

In my defense, while everyone else was kicking and brawling, somebody had to chronicle these developments for future generations to enjoy. It wasn't inaction on my part, therefore. It was a battle cry for posterity. You can't forget about posterity.

But people do forget. In this instance, the kickers and brawlers had forgotten about the beard. Like myself, the head Czech had failed to join in on his men's petty skirmishing. Unlike myself, he was smiling, and the reason he smiled, while I simply gaped, was he had taken out his own pistol. This he now leveled at my left eyebrow.

It was at this juncture that I decided that my inaction—while necessary to achieve the perfect bystander's point of view—might not be all that it was cracked up to be.

Posterity could bite it. I had a gun in my face.

23 — His Way

Slowly and reluctantly, those who had snatched a weapon returned said piece to the bloody-nosed or ruffled-jacketed thug of their choice. I was peeved to see Hutton taking his time over it. His body language implied that watching his best friend receive a bullet to the brain would have been tough, but relinquishing his roscoe was a real wrench.

Once the transactions were complete and the balance sheet of firearms back on par, the beard lowered his gun and laughed. He was a cheerful soul.

"Ha, ha!" he roared—only with a Czech accent. "I knew that you would reveal your true self if so motivated!" He wagged his head at Sergei Brodovitch. "Do you still maintain that you are not the man I think you are?"

Sergei said no. No, he did not—and just like that I realized *he* wasn't speaking in any kind of accent. Not Czech anyway. What gave?

"What do you want?" he asked.

"You know what I want."

"Fine. You got me. Just leave these people alone."

"I cannot do that," said the beard. "I will need to bring along one of them as insurance." He snagged Lesley by the arm. "And the dog," he added. For his trouble.

My strangled gurgle was drowned out by Sergei's rich Midwestern baritone. "No deal!" he growled.

"Ah, but I make it the deal," said the one-and-true Czech. "I have the feeling, with your lovely along with us, you will not make any of the desperate maneuvers for which you are so well known."

"She isn't my lovely!" Sergei objected, and I was right there with him. *You tell 'em, SB,* I might have said, had I been able to speak. "I only met her today," said the phenom.

"Come, come," smiled the beard. "You suspect me of believing that?"

"It's true!" I vociferated, finding the words.

"Who is this?"

Who was I? *Who was I?* The two of us had had a five-minute conversation! He had pointed a gun at my head! Did he mean to tell me that he was only now noticing I was there? "I'm the lovely's fiancé!"

The beard appeared to be having trouble understanding me. His English was not always so good, he said.

"I am her fiancé," I stated again, speaking nice and slow. "We are going to be married."

The beard looked from me to Lesley, then from Lesley back to Sergei Brodovitch. "Surely not," he frowned. He settled on Lesley. "Is this true, *holka*?"

The *holka* nodded. It was true. I would have liked a little more enthusiasm on her part, but at least she didn't deny it.

The beard threw his head back toward the tin ceiling and laughed. Now he had heard everything!

"So you don't need to involve her," said Sergei. "She's nothing to me," he grunted—it was the best grunt I had heard all day.

His ex-boss wasn't so sure. He tallied up the totals. He had his delinquent employee—whatever that was all about. He had a dog. But was it enough? "I think—" he began.

"How about this—" I blurted out.

The beard gawked at me. If he asked me who I was again, so help me, I would not be responsible for my actions.

"How about what?" he wondered.

It was a desperate maneuver I had in mind—Sergei wasn't the only one known for them—but I had to do something. Already I could see the scales tipping rapidly away from the happy ending.

"Are you a musical man at all?" I asked him. I suspected he was.

"I am, yes. Why do you ask this?"

"How would you feel about getting your hands on the missing Romanian Rhapsody of George Enescu. 'Romanian Rhapsody Number Three.' "

I had gotten his attention. Finally. "Romanian Rhapsody, you say?"

" 'Romanian Rhapsody Number Three,' " I emphasized.

The beard pondered. "It is of interest what you say. I am not, myself, so partial to the music of Romania. It is not Czech Republic—but this discovery, it would be what you call, a feather in my head, right?"

A giant feather, I agreed.

"Something to hold over your Romanian friends," Ate suggested.

"Great at cocktail parties," Hutton remarked.

The man was coming around. "You can get me this piece?"

I said I could. For a price. "Our freedom."

His nod suggested that this was a reasonable trade. "Where is this rhapsody now?"

"A friend has it. Enescu Fleet."

"I have heard of this man Enescu Fleet."

I said yeah—who hadn't? "He brings us the score, and then you let us all go. All of us."

"Including Sergei," stuck in Lesley.

I shook my head. Girls have no sense of when to broach these subjects.

As I suspected, we had gone too far. The beard bridled. "No, I think that is not what we will do," he retorted. "I shall have the rhapsody and the man you know as Sergei Brodovitch, and I shall have the fiancée as the insurance!" The henchmen whispered in his ear. He nodded. "And the dog," he agreed. Might as well make a clean sweep of it.

I could be wrong, but I'm not certain we got such a hot deal there.

Fifteen minutes later, the five of us sat on the floor in the corner—Ate, Hutton, Lesley, Sergei and myself. Two of the beard's men had been dispatched to escort Fleet here—by force, if necessary. That left the remaining underlings to diddle about on the other side of the studio.

One was amusing himself by pecking out "Chopsticks" on the piano (not well). The other—looking to win a bet proposed by his compatriot—was attempting to lift his salami-like leg up on the dancer's bar, to the amusement of his employer.

Sergei was the first to speak in our little circle. Leaning the back of his head against the wainscoting, he said, "You two shouldn't have tried to buy my freedom. You should have just offered the missing score for the four of you and left it at that. It was a clever ploy until then."

I half smiled. Showed what he knew. It wasn't nearly that clever. "We weren't going anywhere anyway. There is no score."

He lifted his head off the paneling. "No score?"

"Not that we know of. If there is one, Enescu Fleet doesn't have it."

"Then why did you say that he had?"

"You gotta say something."

"That's Hath," Hutton chimed in. "Always thinking."

I glared. "It bought us some time, didn't it?"

Hutton supposed it did. That was the nice thing about Hutton: when the chips were down, you could always depend on his support, even if your plan was hopeless.

Ate, not so persuaded, wondered what good it would do us, delaying the chop. Lesley tapped my knee and told me that I had tried my best; that was the important thing.

We returned to our brooding silence. Across the studio, Prague's answer to Baryshnikov yowled in pain. He never should have tried any leg exercises after the girls had worked the groin.

"I'm not so sure that it was so stupid," Sergei spoke up suddenly.

"Huh?" asked the four of us.

"I'm not so sure that it was such a stupid ploy," he said. I was beginning to like this man.

"What do you mean?" Lesley asked.

"If Fleet is the man everyone says he is, we might just have enough muscle to carry it through this time. The problem before," he said, "was we were outgunned. We came up a man short."

I went around the circle, counting. I wondered if he considered me the man short. I squinted irritably as Sergei proceeded:

"With Fleet, we can definitely overpower them."

Once more I asked myself if he counted me as one of the "we."

"It seems like you've been in some pretty tight spots before," Hutton suggested.

Sergei shrugged. "A few, yes."

"I take it you're not a piano student, then?"

"Not exactly. I used to be—well, let's just say I had a slightly different line of work."

"Ex-CIA?"

"Something like that."

Hutton had thought as much. "So how'd you end up here?"

"Long story."

Hutton thought it might be. "How about the short version?"

The company man marshaled his thoughts. The short version was, after years of service, Sergei Brodovitch had allowed the pressure of his job to finally get to him. He bugged out. After disappearing off the grid, he wound up on the doorstep of his original handler, Lyle Pendleton.

Hutton held up a hand. "Hold the line. Old Lyle was Agency too?" He sniffed amusedly. After all this, it wouldn't have surprised him to learn that Chester Callas had actually been MI-6. "So Lyle Pendleton gave you sanctuary at the college?"

"He did everything for me. He gave me a false transcript, a backstory, everything. It was his idea that I pose as a Czech exchange student. He even came up with the name."

"You mean, you're not really Sergei Brodovitch?" Lesley asked.

That's right, I thought—let's remove some of that glamour!

Sergei—or perhaps not Sergei—shook his head. "Nope. My real name's Steve Brody. Just a poor farm boy from the Midwest trying to find his way in the world."

I slumped lower. "Steve Brody" was every bit as glamorous as "Sergei Brodovitch." Maybe more glamorous. When it comes to cool, you can't beat a Steve.

"I never cared for the Czech-ifying of it," he admitted. "*Sergei Brodovitch*—it doesn't exactly roll off the tongue."

"It does sound kind of Russian," Ate said.

"I know, right? Totally Russian. But I had to trust Lyle's instincts. They never let me down before. In the end, everyone at the college seemed to accept me. I've blended in pretty smoothly here."

"I guess you had to learn to play the piano at some point?" commented Hutton.

"I already knew how to do that. The piano was my cover. The agency likes you to use your natural talents whenever possible. Play to your strengths. The problem was, those strengths were a little too strong, I think. They got me noticed."

"And that's how the Czech mob caught up with you?" Lesley assumed.

Steve nodded. "Except they're not mob. That was just a false rumor that grew out of the real facts. The colonel is ex-Czech military. He runs a security company that's really more of a small private army. He functions mostly out of South America, but he strays up here every once in a while when he needs to find some new clients."

"Colonel?" I asked. It amazed me that a man that furry of face could have ever made it past lieutenant.

"Colonel Smith," whispered Steve Brody.

"Colonel *Smith*?"

"That's what they call him. Apparently his Czech name is completely unpronounceable. The natives took to referring to him as Smith, and it stuck."

"Keeps things simple," Hutton agreed. He glanced across the studio, frowning. "He does seem rather obsessed with you?"

Steve supposed he was. "We first met in a club he ran in Argentina. I was under a different alias then, working as a waiter who had emigrated from Chile. I used to play the piano in the lounge on slow nights, and sometimes I'd go off on these classical riffs. They impressed him. He offered me a job with the national orchestra, but I turned him down. It wouldn't have fit my mission. Then there was this set-to with an up-and-coming dictator, also not my mission, and my cover got blown."

"What kind of set-to?" wondered Lesley.

"A firefight."

"Oo."

"The dictator didn't make it out alive."

"Ah."

"That's when I beat it. I couldn't do it anymore: living every moment by my wits, finding danger and intrigue wherever I went. I couldn't do it."

Lesley batted her eyelids mellowly, and I frowned, not so mellowly. *Tone it down, Steve,* I might have said, *tone it down.* He already had one obsessive fan; he didn't need another.

"When the colonel learned about my hidden talents, he had to have me back on his staff. I could be one part muscle, one part corps musician."

"Then he really does want you as his pianist?" I said.

"Pretty much. I'm not sure I wouldn't rather he killed me."

They were both good options, I conceded.

One thing still puzzled me: "Why'd you kidnap Pixie?"

This was another long story, Steve grumbled.

As before, he accommodated us with the abridged version. After Lyle wound up dead, he didn't know where to turn. Already his cover was in jeopardy because of the fame he had achieved at the college, and the murder investigations weren't helping. He had to find an ally. He knew Enescu Fleet by reputation, but he didn't know if he could trust him, or even if he was the real Enescu Fleet. Impostors were a way of life for Steve Brody. Also, he thought he had heard something a while back about a fake Fleet working in the industry.

(Hutton smiled sheepishly.)

"After Chester Callas was killed, I tried to ask Lyle about him, but we were interrupted at his villa before I could confirm Fleet's identity."

Hutton smiled sheepishly a second time. That would have been his fault, he said. Steve told him not to worry about it.

"When Lyle got murdered, I didn't know what to think. I didn't want to reveal too much, but I had to arrange a meeting with Fleet. I had a girl I know bring his dog to me, and then I left him that message. I figured if Fleet was the man he claimed to be, he would find me. I knew he excelled at code cracking. And a true Romanian would know about the calendar differences."

"Or, in our case, honorary Romanians would," said Hutton. "By the way, Fleet isn't one either."

"Not Romanian?"

"Not so much, no."

"But he claims to be a descendent of George Enescu?"

"Another of Lyle Pendleton's little ideas," I explained.

"Well, I'll be," said Steve Brody.

I don't know what he was griping about. It's the same thing Lyle and he had done to us. The *L* man could be a real scallywag.

"Anyway, it was some puzzle you gave us," Hutton commended him. "Is that something they teach you in spy school?"

The ex-spy wasn't listening. "What's that? No, not really."

"Well, it was inspired. What made you think of using a date as a code?"

Brody thought about it. "It was something Lyle Pendleton said. When I went to his villa today and started to ask him about Fleet, he answered with a question of his own. He asked me when I write out a date, do I list the month first or the day. I told him I list the month first. He nodded and told me that in Europe they list the day first. Then he chuckled. I don't think I had ever seen him chuckle. I'm not sure I had ever seen him smile. He chuckled again and said *the date, of course.* I asked him what was the date, and he said the clue—*the clue was a date.* Then he asked if I knew the internal extensions on campus. I said I didn't, and that's when you arrived. That's what made me think of using a date as a code."

The four of us looked between us. The extensions again. Lyle was onto something with the extensions. One of them had something to do with a date. That's what Chester Callas was trying to tell us.

"Anyone know any significant dates for Frank Sinatra?" Ate asked.

No one did.

"If an extension represented a date to Chester," said Hutton, "with the day first, the month second and the year last, then it would have to have been a significant date in 1932, 1936, 1956, 1985 or 1986." He had a pretty good memory himself.

"When was Sinatra married?" asked Lesley.

"Which time?" Ate replied.

"Any of the times. Were any of them during those years?"

No one knew.

Ate heaved a sigh. "Guess we need Dad for that too. Those bastards took our phones, or we could just look up the answer online."

Steve perked up. "Your dad's pretty knowledgeable?"

"He once spent three months on a desert island reading a complete encyclopedia. If you'd call that knowledgeable."

He blinked at her. "He read a whole encyclopedia on an island?"

"The volumes washed up on shore with him after his ship had wrecked. What else was he going to do with them?"

Steve nodded slowly.

We would have to shelve the Sinatra dates for now. It was just as well. I had more pressing matters on my mind. "So how'd *you* wind up here?" I asked Lesley.

She looked my way. She may have forgotten I was there. "After I finished renting the hall for the wedding, I saw a girl taking Pixie into this building. I got curious. I followed them up here, and that's when Sergei, or rather Steve, told me he was in trouble. He was just explaining everything when you all came in."

I sniffed. *Explaining*—is that what they called it? "And how much *explaining* would you all have done had we *not* come in?"

She didn't get a chance to answer this question, because just then another set of people came in. The colonel's men had returned. Enescu Fleet wasn't among them.

A lack of Fleet wasn't the only thing that impressed itself on us. Their knobby skulls were scuffed and grazed, like someone had been practicing stickball with them. One of the men favored his left foot, while the other showed a distinct aversion to lifting his right arm.

Both had fat lips.

Not surprisingly, an impromptu discussion kicked off here in noisy Czech. Steve Brody obliged us by translating:

"They found Enescu Fleet alright," he said. "They asked him if they could have a word with him. Fleet agreed, and they took a stroll down an alley. Apparently one of them...there seems to be some dispute which one...made an injudicious remark. Fleet became suspicious. The men tried to strong-arm him...Something about a blur of tweed...That's all I got."

I had mixed emotions hearing this. On one hand, I felt, *Good for you, Ef.* On the other, what did this mean for us?

Steve had the answer to this as well. Steve had the answer to everything. "Before sending them on their way, Fleet got some information out of them. He knows about us."

"Is that what they're yelling about?" I asked.

"That's what they're yelling about," he replied.

After a space of additional shouting, more thunderous than any piano playing from Sergei Brodovitch, the colonel smoothed his necktie, spat on the hardwood floor and came to converse with us. He spoke in a suppressed rumble.

"It seems Enescu Fleet wishes to negotiate your release. He insists on doing this on his own terms. He will not involve the authorities, he says, provided that I hand you all over to him. He suspects, correctly, that I would not agree to this, and so he has offered to have one of you act as a go-between, so that we can come to an agreement. I am to send the one called Johnny Hathaway, the well-known freelance courier, to the Pendleton Library, together with the dog known as Pixie."

Ate snorted. She always knew Dad liked her best.

"The one called Hathaway shall bring a page of the rhapsody back to me as a show of good faith. I will then release another captive, whereupon Enescu Fleet will send Hathaway here with the entire score, along with the *passports*"—he glared back at his battered associates—"Enescu Fleet managed to take off my men. Up, John Hathaway."

I upped.

I didn't much like the idea of acting as a go-between, but I suppose when you're a world-famous freelance courier, you have to give the people what they want.

Colonel S. handed me Pixie, and off I went.

Thanks to the bastard Brody, I had Rachmaninoff stuck in my head now. Or it may have been the "Minute Waltz." I was humming it to Pixie as I carried her along the path between the two buildings, trying to keep my nerves intact and my eyes on the prize. In other words, I wasn't paying attention. No sooner had I passed out of view of the Cabriole than I felt a hand on my shoulder and a pointy object pressing against my back. A voice whispered, "This way, daddy-o. Got a detour for you."

I knew that diction. Apparently Henry Pratt—and what felt like the sharpened piccolo I had described to Rachel Barton Pine earlier—would be accompanying us on our march.

Personally I would have preferred to go *a cappella*.

24 — Banding Together

He was right about the detour. He forced me off the path, across an empty parking lot, over a field of grass, and ultimately through the basement door of one of the less glamorous buildings on the Pendleton campus. It reminded me of a gymnasium from the seventies.

Over the last leg of the journey, Pixie had begun to shift and grumble in my arms, plainly taking exception to this rough transport. I could appreciate her resentment. I, myself, enjoyed evening strolls much more when someone wasn't pushing a stiletto into my back.

Once inside, Pratt shoved me down a hall and into a room, both of which smelled of seventies gym. He hit the lights. They buzzed and clicked overhead, reluctant to comply; then with a cough and a gasp, they flickered on, becoming a consistent, yellowish hue.

We were in a kind of band storage closet now: a long, narrow space so full of percussion and brass that one good sneeze would have sounded like the spontaneous combustion of "Seventy-Six Trombones."

Pratt, I saw, wasn't looking his best either, not that he ever did. The two-day growth on his face had moved past the cool-cat phase and was rapidly approaching skid-row bum. His uniform was sweaty and ragged, and the trilby atop his head lacked the proper jauntiness.

He looked like hell.

I observed a workbench on my right, used for instrument repair. I set Pixie down on this, alongside a tuba in need of a new set of struts and shocks. I stretched my back.

"That's enough of that," he said, reapplying the spear.

I ceased stretching. Peering back, I caught a glimpse of the prod. It consisted of a pointed baton—metal—not the sawed-off piccolo I had originally envisaged. It wasn't the twirling kind of baton—that would have made too much sense—but the long, thin kind, such as conductors enjoy rapping on their podiums.

I wouldn't have wanted it shoved through my guts if I could help it, but it didn't look nearly as lethal as it felt.

"What now, sport?" I asked him.

Pratt didn't care for my use of his lingo.

"Enough with the *sport*," he sneered—or a sneer was what it sounded like; my back was still to him. "So let's have it," he demanded.

"Let's have what?"

"The score."

"The score?" I would have thought it obvious that I had no inkling what the score was.

"The *score* score," said Pratt. "Romanian Rhapsody Part Three. I have a buyer for it, and I know one of you has it."

"Not I." For the second time in as many minutes, I felt Henry Pratt's hands all over me. It wasn't pleasant.

"Okay, maybe you don't have it on you."

"Exactly as I've been telling you."

"But that doesn't mean you don't have it. Somebody has to have it."

I wasn't sure somebody did. "Can I go now?" I asked.

"No, you can't go!" Pratt shouted. He had an effective voice. It was too bad marching bands didn't need vocalists; he'd have a real future.

He explained the situation: "I left word for the rest of the band to meet me outside. They're going to help get me out of town. Kenny's sister has this place…never you mind where Kenny's sister's place is," he growled, prodding the flesh.

I didn't mind. I didn't even know who Kenny was. "You going on the lam?"

"That's right. Wouldn't you, with a murder rap staring you in the mug?"

"Perhaps," I said; although I never much cared for travel. I always seem to run into the wrong sort of people. "So what do you need me for?"

"You're my insurance."

More with the insurance! Lesley was insurance; I was insurance; everyone's insurance. Were we wearing Prudential T-shirts?

"You're going to help me get out of this unscathed."

I doubted that. I had never helped anyone get out of anything unscathed before; I saw no reason why I should start now. "So it was you all along. You French-horned Lyle Pendleton. You rub out Chet Callas too?"

"I didn't rub out anyone, man. Not Lyle, not the Brit, no one. I just did what I was told."

"Yeah, and what was that?"

"Never you mind."

I was beginning to detect a theme here. "Why don't you tell the police that you didn't do it?"

I heard him guffaw. "Who are the cops gonna believe, a two-bit band student from the wrong side of the tracks or—" He prodded my back again. "Never you mind who they aren't going to believe."

I could see I wasn't going to get anywhere appealing to Pratt's better side. His better side wasn't all that good.

I shuffled forward again—thinking, thinking.

"You sit tight here," he muttered, guiding me to the back. It somehow managed to be both darker and more yellowish than the rest of the room. "I'm gonna go see if the boys are back yet."

I ceased thinking. I knew what had to be done. If my recent inaction in the dance studio taught me anything, it was that it never pays to be a wallflower. Inaction, bad. Action, good. (Also, if you want to model yourself on Steve Brody, a sharp elbow to the jaw does wonders toward asserting your personality.)

Waiting until the moment was right, which apparently it was—or as right as it ever was going to be—I jerked back and elbowed with all I had. The element of surprise: that's the ticket in these situations.

There was definitely plenty of surprise. No doubt about that. Unfortunately, a good deal of this was on my part. In one smooth motion my mighty elbow flew through the air, whizzed past Henry Pratt's mug and connected with the wall of shelves behind us.

Ask anyone who has ever knocked into a mounted shelf and they can guess the upshot here—in fact, ask anyone who has ever tried to assemble a mounted shelf and they can guess. It sprang up like an elephant landing on a seesaw. The spronging shelf struck another shelf; that shelf, now also spronging, slipped loose and smacked into the shelves above it; and two seconds later, a deluge of band instruments came crashing down on our heads.

It wasn't pleasant to hear, and it didn't feel much better.

I tried to get out of the way, but something whacked me in the head before I could. I think it was a tambourine. I staggered back and watched as Henry Pratt disappeared behind a cascade of drumsticks.

There was plenty of dust after that, and for a minute Pratt and I occupied ourselves with coughing and hacking. He hacked; I coughed.

I finished up first and set my feet. We stood facing each other. I was pleased to see that he had dropped his baton. It was just the two of us now, mano a bando. He lunged.

After an initial engagement, I stepped back and assessed the situation. I liked my chances. There was a hesitance about the way he jabbed and pawed at me, which I found very encouraging.

"You want to hit me," I goaded him, "hit me."

He jutted forward again, snatching me by the shirt and flinging me into the wall. He answered in the negative: "No punching. A musician has to protect his hands."

"You play the *drums*," I snapped.

He scowled. I had wounded him.

He grabbed me around the collar, and I grabbed him around the collar, and we twirled and twirled until I somehow wound up bouncing off the wall again, and he landed on a pile of used epaulettes.

Pixie was there, still on her table, dusty but otherwise none the worse for wear.

"Woof!" she remarked. I like to think it was a woof of encouragement.

"Had enough?" he asked, rising up from the tassels.

I hadn't. As far as I could make out, I had him right where I wanted him. You wouldn't know it by watching us, but this more or less played into my wheelhouse. I don't like to brag, but on the field of battle I had one thing I could be proud of. I could take a punch. Hutton might have his catlike reflexes; Fleet a remarkable upper body and those aged fists of fury. I had this. I'm not saying I had a granite jaw or anything, but a Henry Pratt with essentially two hands tied behind his back, I could manage.

He lurched forward again and ensnared the polo. I slipped the grip and landed a nice blow on his mouth, which may well have been granite. He lurched and ensnared once more, and I stuck the jab and landed another power punch. He didn't budge. He lurched a third time, but before I could stick or punch, he head-butted me.

The head. I hadn't considered the head. If there's one thing a drummer doesn't care about, it's his head.

I reeled back. Pratt charged forward for another knock, but I reached out and stiff-armed him in his doughy face. That's when he stepped into my trap. In a stunning lapse of prudence, he hit me. One clenched fist, no waiting. It landed squarely on my forehead, the last place he would have aimed for.

Bone struck bone. The thud reverberated through the storage room, and so did Henry Pratt's expletive.

Don't get me wrong; it stung on my end too, but he got the worst of it. I toppled back, dazed, while he staggered forward, massaging his knuckles.

"Did you break it?" I asked.

"Don't think so," he said.

"Good," I replied. I kicked him in the kneecap.

He cursed again. I jumped up, wishing I hadn't soared to my feet quite so fast. Regaining my bearings, I tackled him across the midriff. We toppled over, and his head got driven into the wall.

I suppose I drove it there.

We lay sprawled out on the concrete floor a moment. He was breathing—which should have pleased him—but other than that, he didn't have much going for him. I had described him earlier as not looking his best. His previous not best was parsecs beyond this not best.

I climbed up out of the clutter and stretched my back (see him give me a hard time about that now).

The important thing was, Pixie had enjoyed herself. She was treading the table with the pent-up excitement of a Maltese who has just witnessed the brawl of the year.

She woofed again, this time unmistakably encouraging, and I raked her in and undid the leash from her collar.

I tied up Henry Pratt with this, just his hands, and dragged him to his feet. He was woozy but conscious. As we marched out, I hoicked his trilby off the floor and put it on my head. He wouldn't need it where he was going.

We narrowly avoided running into his compadres on our way out the door. A mob of them had begun to pour in from the empty parking lot across the street. Ate and Hutton were right: they looked like a bunch of hooligans.

A little fancy footwork on my part and my prisoner and I were up the path and out of view before anyone saw us.

I was happy not to bump into anyone else on our way to the Pendleton Library. It's never easy to explain why you and the school's bandleader are battered and bruised, the bandleader is tied up with a dog leash, and you're carrying a dusty Maltese. Fortunately, the trail went smoothly, as did the alley behind the library and the walkway to the back entrance.

There we hit a small obstacle. A horde of concertgoers, heavy metal fans from the look of them, were blocking our path. Most of them had their backs to us, but those who did look our way didn't seem bothered by our battle scars or Pratt's restraints. Leather leashes were all status quo to them.

Suddenly the mob parted, and a woman emerged.

I had barely time to open the door to the basement, shove Henry Pratt across the threshold and toss Pixie in after him before the newcomer called to me.

"Is that John Hathaway?" she said.

I stepped a little closer, still holding a portion of the "leash cuffs" through the crevice of the shut door. Pratt wasn't going anywhere.

The woman certainly commanded attention. Bright red lipstick, a rough black dress complete with chrome studs, snake necklace—I think it was a snake—spiked wristbands, non-spiked wristbands, lace driving gloves and all the fixings.

I focused in closer, and recognition dawned. If it weren't for the violin case, I wouldn't have recognized her.

The woman was Rachel Barton Pine. And yet it wasn't Rachel Barton Pine. How hard had Pratt hit me?

"Nice to see you again, John."

I said uh. Or it might have been heh.

"Actually, I'm glad we bumped into each other," she remarked.

"Heh," I agreed, unless it was "Uh."

"Earthen Grave takes the stage in a few minutes, but I wanted to tell you something."

Earthen Grave. Of course! Now I understood. I had seen posters around campus for a heavy metal band, featuring, among other things, a heavy metal violin. So Rachel was the violin. She was a woman of many talents.

"I wanted to tell you something about Frank Sinatra."

I came out of my reverie. It wasn't only the mention of the dying clue. Behind the door Henry Pratt had just tugged at his restraints, pulling my face into the frame.

"Are you quite alright?" Rachel asked.

I said I was. "You were saying something about Frank Sinatra?"

"Yes. I didn't think about it until I was warming up backstage, but there's a different meaning to that name. *Frank Sinatra* is sometimes used as a nickname for Franck's *Sonata in A.*"

"Franck's *Sonata in A*?"

"César Franck's *Sonata for Violin and Piano*. The Franck Sonata."

"In *A*?"

"In *A*," she agreed.

"So people call the Franck Sonata, Frank Sinatra?" I said.

She nodded. "I never actually called it that myself, but a few years ago I was doing an interview with an author and he mentioned that violin students sometimes refer to it as that as a sort of humorous shorthand. I thought it was funny."

I thought it pretty amusing myself. "Frank's Sonata."

"*Franck*," she corrected.

"Franck," I replied, bouncing off the door again.

"Franck."

I had it. *Franck.* "So that's what Chester Callas meant when he said Frank Sinatra?"

"It's possible. At any rate, I thought it might help."

It had, I told her, it had.

"You'll pass it along to Fleet?"

I told her I would, I would.

"Thanks. Nice hat," she said, and left.

One more carom into the doorframe, and I headed inside myself.

Any concerns I might have had that Henry Pratt could be suffering from a concussion and would do well to seek a good noggin specialist were alleviated during our extended trek up the stairs to the main library. No one with any trauma to the brainpan could have weaved together such an impressive string of obscenities as he did. His use of four-letter words together with street jargon from both the 1950s and the present would have astonished you.

These musicians, they all seem to have a multitude of skills.

Thankfully, our walking tour wasn't prolonged. I spotted the Ef man as soon as we came in. He was standing in the middle of the room, the glow of the skylight beaming down on his thoughtful features. He was accompanied by Nathaniel Goody, Dean of Pendleton College; Victoria Walters, Orchestral Director; and Tanya Saxon, Tough Old Broad.

Our arrival went over big. You'd have thought they had never seen a bound-up band drummer before.

Fleet held up his hand to silence the din. He had that kind of power over people. The other hand went to stroking his musty Maltese. "Are you alright, Johnny?"

It was nice that somebody asked. I told him I was fine.

"Cool beans. Now then, what kept you?"

I shot Pratt a look. The latter was wriggling on a chair, working out the finer points of his next harangue.

I gave Fleet a short synopsis of our afternoon.

I started with the Pixie-napping, moved on to the secret world of Sergei Brodovitch, and wrapped up with Henry Pratt's Hathaway-napping.

"Oh, and Rachel Barton Pine said hello."

Fleet smiled handsomely. "It's always nice to hear from Rachel."

"She said—oh jeez!"

As you know, that's not what she said. Something had just occurred to me. It hit me like a flying tambourine to the head.

"I'm supposed to be helping free Lesley, Hutton and your daughter! By now—"

Fleet waved another airy hand. I could see why it worked so well. It was hypnotic.

"That's all taken care of."

"Taken care of?"

"It's fine. Everything proceeded according to plan. They will be with us presently."

They would? I didn't see how. But then again, I had learned not to question Fleet and his waves.

"What did Rachel tell you?" he asked.

His voice was so soothing that I put the girls and Hutton on the back burner. I relayed the facts without further delay.

I told him about the Frank Sinatra, the Franck Sonata and Rachel's dress.

Fleet's smile became handsomer. "Finally, a breakthrough. With any luck we should know the murderer's identity in no time."

I was less enthused. "Then Henry Pratt was telling the truth? He's not the killer?"

"I'm sorry, no. Involved in the crimes, yes; killer, no."

I had figured as much. If I had learned anything else associating with Enescu Fleet these last few years, it was that the muscle never turned out to be the culprit. It was too easy.

"So who did it?"

"Yes," replied Fleet.

Was that it? *Yes.* "Don't you know?" I wondered.

I would have thought the answer obvious. I mean, it wasn't to me—it never was—but for a man of his talents it should be.

Chester had spoken of Frank Sinatra, which we now knew referred to César Franck's *Violin Sonata in A*. All that was required, then, was to draw upon that vast encyclopedic knowledge of Fleet's, gained from reading twenty-six volumes on a desert island, and we'd have it. Fleet had said it himself: there was something in those phone extensions.

One of them was the last thing Chet Callas saw before he died, five digits that somehow connected with Franck's Sonata and, by association, the murderer.

"What was the hold up?" I asked.

Fleet ushered us away from the faculty. "The fact is, Johnny, there's a hiccup in my vast knowledge."

"A what?"

"A hiccup."

I frowned. "You never read a complete encyclopedia on a desert island, did you? There was no desert island. You've never even been to sea, have you?"

"I did, there was and I have. But the set wasn't complete."

"How not complete?"

"It was absent one volume."

I could guess what this one volume was. "The *F*?"

"The *F*," said Enescu Fleet. There was something fitting about that. Ef missing his *F*. It put one in mind of Greek mythology.

"Then you don't know much about César Franck?"

"Not so much as nothing."

"Fantastic," I said. That was fantastic with an *F*.

Any additional wry retorts I might have made would have to go un-retorted for now. There was a clang in the back of the room, and our friends filed in.

I was delighted to see them, but also puzzled. There was a formality to the way they marched in and congregated around the desks.

Henry Pratt might have appreciated it, but not I.

Steve Brody, alias Brodovitch, came in first, then Lesley, Ate and Hutton. The Czech contingent followed but with a sole representative: Colonel Smith. Smith's men, the Bubblehead Four, had not joined us.

There was one other traveler with the pack. From behind Smith, a figure stepped out holding a gun. He had been concealed behind the colonel, applying the weapon as a prod.

The Pratt maneuver. I of all people should have spotted that one.

The second set of feet should have also tipped us off. Very few colonels have four legs.

I had no difficulty in recognizing the figure now. I didn't know his name, or even if he had a name. But I knew what I called him.

The Romanian.

25 — High Note

Casting a wary eye back at the colonel, he stepped around, giving us all a hard look. He then progressed to where Fleet was standing. For Ef, he reserved the hardest gaze of all.

Fleet returned it with his own private blend of stolid congeniality: the sort of look that made him both an effective detective and a man who, when he dined out in the evening, could always get a table by the window. They held their stare-down for another ten seconds, at which point the Romanian relaxed his grip on his weapon and made a slight bow in Fleet's direction.

Fleet returned this as well, more of a nod than a bow, but every bit as respectful. "I thank you, sir. I am in your debt."

The Romanian bowed again. Perhaps he was Japanese. He didn't look Japanese.

I had a question. I always had a question. "What the hell?" I asked.

For once, I felt most everyone in the room shared my confusion. Already a grumbling noise had begun to permeate the silent stares, questioning what we had just seen.

Fleet had an explanation. Fleet always had an explanation.

"Ladies and gentlemen, earlier today my daughter and several friends were forcibly detained in a dance studio on campus. This man helped extract them."

The announcement went over well. Nobody, I'm sure, had a freaking clue what was going on—not even myself, and I was one of the several friends—but we correctly interpreted this as good news. Nate Goody said, "Excellent work." Tanya Saxon seconded the sentiment. Victoria Walters started to clap her hands, then appeared to think better of it and smiled.

I looked over at the other gathering, now headed by Ate.

I wasn't certain if they had known about their extraction or not—their blank expressions suggested not—but they got into the spirit of the congratulations now. Ate looked the most pleased: due in no small part, I would bet, to her father describing the detainees as *his daughter and friends*, and not *his dog Pixie and some human acquaintances*.

"So you were in league with the man all along," I said, beginning to see daylight. "That's why, when I saw him following us at the concert, I didn't have to identify him to you. You knew who I was indicating before I had even pointed him out."

My deduction earned another bow. It was like a big night on Broadway, this place. "True. And once again, excellent detective work. You're coming along nicely on that."

I thanked him, if you call a wry snort a thank you. "When did you join forces?"

"Earlier today, when the man approached me with a view to helping him secure the missing Romanian Rhapsody for return to his home government."

The missing Romanian Rhapsody. I had almost forgotten about that. But was there a missing rhapsody? I couldn't keep track. "Then he *is* Romanian?"

"Indeed."

"Ha!" Another one right. "Doesn't talk much, does he?"

"No, Johnny, he does not. His understanding of English is first-rate, but he feels his pronunciation lacks polish. He only speaks when he feels he must."

This made a change from my regular circle. Most of them only shut up when they feel they must. "I guess he has military training."

"Quite extensive, yes."

I nodded. His handiwork with the trombone would have told me that. I smiled to myself. A more thorough pack of battle-trained music lovers I had never come across. "Lucky he was available."

"His presence here came about more naturally than you might think. He and Mr. Brody have worked together before."

I glanced at Brody and then back to the Romanian. It was my turn to say, *Well, I'll be.*

"You know each other?"

Steve confirmed this. They had worked a few assignments together in the old days. "Apparently he's been trying to catch up with me all weekend. When his government sent him here, he recognized my photo somewhere and wanted to solicit my help. But we kept missing each other. I was as amazed as anyone when he appeared in the dance studio."

I made another sniffing sound. It looked like Steve and the gang were no longer a man short. I turned back to Fleet. "So you never intended any kind of swap with the rhapsody? I was just a pawn in your scheme. Actually, I wasn't good enough to be a pawn. I was like one of those spare checker pieces you find in chess sets and fling aside, wondering how it got there."

The schemer frowned. I don't know why it was, but I always seemed to bring out the underlying melancholy in the world for Fleet. "I wouldn't say that, Johnny. You are and always will be integral to my plans. In this case, I needed to remove you simply because you knew the man by sight and might complicate the rescue with an inadvertent comment. By the same token, I had you remove Pixie because she had also tangled with him and is of an excitable disposition, never one to think before she acts."

I nodded again and gave another snort. I understood. When you have a delicate maneuver in the works, it always helps to clear the board of dogs and idiots.

"I hope my actions did not wound your feelings."

I waved it off. I was used to it.

That all settled, Fleet fixed Colonel Smith in a steady gaze. This time, there was no congeniality in his stare. In fact, I had never seen him look so intense.

"You are aware," he informed the Czech, "that my treatment of your employees when they came to collect me was only a tiny glimpse into what I would have done to you had any harm come to my daughter, my dog or our friends. No private army in the world would have stood between us."

The colonel gestured apologetically. He assured us that he had no doubts about Fleet's ability to get a job done. This was borne in upon him the moment he saw his four soldiers lying unconscious at his feet with tranquilizer darts in their throats. It was more borne, he said, when he felt Fleet's Romanian emissary pressing a semiauto pistol into the base of his skull.

"Just so you understand, then," said Fleet.

The colonel understood. "This was all a misunderstanding. I only wished to establish contact with Sergei Brodovitch and offer him work. That is all."

"You're done making job offers. These aren't some Eastern European badlands where people get scooped up from their homes in the middle of the night and dragooned into service."

"No? No, of course not. If a man doesn't want to work, you can't make him work," said the colonel. "I will find others who wish to fill the void in the free-market system." He peered toward the Romanian. "If, by chance, you ever find yourself at a loose end..." he started to say. "No, no," he decided. "We can discuss it some other time, perhaps."

Victoria Walters spoke up. "Well, hasn't this been exhilarating!" she smiled. "I'm not exactly sure what has been going on, but it looks like you've saved the day again, Ef." She placed a kindly hand on Brody's shoulder. "I'm delighted you're okay, Sergei."

"Call me Steve."

"I—Oh—I beg your pardon?"

"I suppose we should call it a day," said Tanya Saxon, not concerned with why the pianist had abruptly changed his name to Steve. "I find myself quite exhausted by all this."

Nate Goody supported the call to disperse. "I think we should all have a drink," he declared. "I still have that bottle of tuica in my office somewhere. I had a whole case at one point, but I still haven't located it. I swear people move things on me. It's a damned conspiracy."

Fleet cleared his throat. "I believe there is something we are forgetting here."

"And what is that?" Nate wondered.

"The small matter of a double murder."

"Oh yes. Yes, of course."

"Not to mention the presence of your marching-band leader tied up in the corner with a busted lip."

Nate gazed at Pratt. He had noticed the bandleader earlier; it was true. What was Ef's point?

Victoria had forgotten all about him, she was embarrassed to admit; while Tanya Saxon replied in her dry way that she had assumed that ending up bound and trussed in a library chair was the normal travail of any school-band participant.

She had never supported the program herself.

"As for solving a double murder, Mr. Fleet, there are some things, I think, better left—"

Who Tanya Saxon thought some things were better left to, we weren't privileged to learn. It may have been "the police," or "the birds," or maybe even "that illustrious young man, John P. Hathaway."

We'll never know. The remark had hardly left her pruney lips when a ruckus erupted above us. It started with a coarse cry to arms—followed by what I swear sounded like the tooting of a tiny kazoo—and before you could say *Ladies and Gentlemen, the Pendleton College Marching Band*, Henry Pratt's vermillion-clad brethren had risen up from behind the rails of the second-story catwalks.

There had to be fifteen of them, easy, each more hard-bitten than the last, and in every hand a bottle. The bottle in the hand closest to us was topped with a flaming wick.

"What's he holding?" Lesley asked.

"Some sort of Molotov cocktail," answered Hutton.

Everybody knows about the Molotov. You fling a flaming bottle of some combustible substance toward your opponent, the bottle breaks, and *blam!* I consider myself an expert on cocktails, and this wasn't the proper use of the ingredients at all.

Dean Goody was squinting up at the bottles. "Is that my tuica?" he called up to them. He turned to me. "I believe they have my tuica."

I was happy for him. The good man had found his tuica.

The hooligan with the flaming wick appeared to be calling the shots. Perhaps this was Kenny, the one whose family had a place outside of town. He looked like a Kenny.

"Everyone freeze!" he yelled, "or we'll burn this place to a cinder." I didn't care for his word mix. Freeze, burn to cinder. You can't have both.

"Nobody move!" shouted another of the band: a girl hooligan this time, with red hair and piercings up and down her freckled face.

"Band rocks!" hollered a man with a greasy mop of hair—not one of the deepest thinkers of the gang.

"We're here for Pratt!" yelled Kenny—let's assume he was Kenny. The words sent a cheer through his compatriots. The bottles danced in their hands.

Out of the chaos, a single, reassuring voice spoke.

"Let's all keep calm here," said Enescu Fleet.

He directed the remark to the Romanian as much as anyone. I could see why. The last thing we needed was an Old West saloon shoot-out, with opponents getting picked off the balcony, tumbling down and bursting into sheets of flame all around us.

"Nobody wants to do anything stupid—"

"Band forever!" hollered Greasy Mop. (Perhaps he was an exception.)

"Give us Pratt!" yelled Kenny.

"Your dog's cute!" shouted the girl hoodlum.

Fleet thanked her. "If we give you Pratt, what assurances do we have that you will leave these people and the building unharmed?"

"We just want Pratt's freedom," espoused Kenny, hiccuping. "That's all any one of us ever wanted. Freedom to perform without a bunch of snobs looking down their noses at us. Freedom from our friends getting railroaded into a murder conviction. Fur-freedom!"

"You throw one of those bottles and freedom is the last thing any of you will ever have," said Fleet emphatically. "Clearly you haven't thought this through."

"Not thinking things through!" cheered the Mop.

Fleet frowned. "Am I correct in assuming that you have all sampled the tuica before coming here? Perhaps sampled quite a lot of it?" A cry of *Tuica rocks!* told him that he had assumed correctly.

He sighed. "I can't do anything about the school's opinion of the band program. Sometimes mockery is the cross heady performers like yourselves have to bear. But if you truly desire to see Henry get a fair shake in the murder investigation, then you need to lay down your bottles now and listen to what I have to say. If you do, the authorities may view this outburst as temporary insanity brought about by overwork and an acute case of tuica-poisoning."

Kenny considered Fleet's offer. "How do we know Pratt will get a *share fake*?"

"A fair shake? You have my word. Now then," he said, gazing up, "that bottle has been burning far too long. I'm concerned for your safety as well as ours. The minute the flame reaches the fluid inside—"

"We've *fought* of that," said Kenny.

"They use controlled wicks!" hollered the Mop. "They can burn for hours."

"Think of them like oil lanterns!" explained the Girl. "Perfectly *slafe*," she slurred. I noticed no one considered them *slafe* enough to get near Kenny, the only one with a lit fuse.

Fleet was satisfied. Not happy, but satisfied. He took a trip around the desks, giving Pixie a pat on the head. "If you give me five minutes, you'll see that nobody is getting railroaded here. Henry is not the killer, and I can prove it."

You would think after a pronouncement like that we would be getting down to business. Not so. He paused again, not to pat Pixie, but to take Hutton aside and whisper something. Hutton nodded and slowly sidled away. He disappeared into the shadows.

Despite the flaming sword of Damocles hanging over their heads, most of the crowd had taken a seat now. I preferred to stand.

"Less than twenty-four hours ago," Fleet began, "a man fell to his death in this very spot." He indicated the spot. It was actually about twenty feet to his left, but I didn't interrupt. He didn't need my help. "Chester Callas, music critic for *Resounding Note* magazine, was murdered. He was not a nice man. He was a man with many enemies. One such enemy lured him to the banquet and killed him."

He paused a third time, moving away from the shadowy corner Hutton had retreated to a minute ago. I stiffened. Hutton had disappeared. Really disappeared. Where he had gone was anyone's guess, but this vanishing act had to be part of Fleet's plan. If he was calling on Hutton for support, he had to be desperate.

I peered around the library. I still couldn't spot him. By now, he could be off rallying reinforcements or, knowing Hutton, attempting to sneak behind enemy lines and single-handedly take out the entire band brigade.

I hoped it was for reinforcements.

I won't say Hutton had no skills in hand-to-hand combat—he excelled at Krav Maga—but he wouldn't have been my first choice as honorary Green Beret. He was no Steve Brody. (He wasn't even Romanian.)

Fleet continued to stall: "Just before he died, Chester left us a clue. He said—Johnny."

I twirled around.

"Tell them the clue that Chester Callas left for us."

I nodded. The clue. I could do that. "Frank Sinatra."

"Frank Sinatra," said Enescu Fleet. "A curious clue. What could it mean?"

"Get on with it!" yelled Kenny.

He clearly had an impatient temperament, and despite what he had told us, I'm not sure he trusted the lack of combustibility of his flaming cocktail. He set the bottle on the floor far from where he was leaning and snarled, "Give us the murderer!"

"Quit stalling!" the Mop agreed.

"Is it a *Mull-stese*?" slurred the Girl. "The dog? Is it Mull-stese?"

Fleet assured her on that point.

He went on: "In order to understand the clue, we have to consider the last thing Chester saw before he died. He did not know the identity of his murderer, but he knew their five-digit phone extension. There are a limited number of extensions that could have been used to phone the library's internal line that evening. I shall now read you the list of those that might have called him."

He reached in his pocket, and the band sighed. He read:

Nathaniel Goody, extension 21336
Tanya Saxon, extension 26986
Victoria Walters, extension 27156
Henry Pratt, extension 31332
Sergei Brodovitch, extension 31385.

He folded up the list and placed it back in his pocket.

"You said Henry didn't do it!" shouted the Mop. Or maybe it was more of a holler.

Fleet ignored his objection. "One of these five people murdered Chester Callas, and when Lyle Pendleton got too close to the truth, they killed him too. One of these five extensions relates to Frank Sinatra. But which one?"

I have no doubt that the band would have turned ugly here. And who could blame them? They didn't have far to go. Fortunately Enescu Fleet's stonewalling had reached its height. Hutton reappeared above us. From what I could see, he hadn't snapped any of the band member's necks, and he didn't have the police with him. He did, however, have position. He was on the balcony level above the hoodlums. That would have been grand, had he any weapon with him or even a firehose, but he didn't. He had a book.

"I think I got something here," he called down from his post.

Fleet welcomed his report. "What did you find?"

"You better take a look yourself. Catch."

Most men are smart enough not to try and catch a 2000-page volume thrown from a third-story balcony, and luckily Enescu Fleet was smarter than most men. Then again, most men are smart enough not to throw the tome in the first place, and sadly I couldn't say that for Hutton.

The book smacked the tile in a poof of dust, its thud about twenty times more rattling than any combined Molotov cocktail. It hadn't landed far from where I was standing—crazy bastard—so I ankled over and gave it a look-see. Apparently I had nearly been cold-cocked by *Baker's Biographical Dictionary of Musicians* (Nick Slonimsky, ed.)

Fleet picked up the volume, turned to the page Hutton had dog-eared and read. Pixie helped.

Time drifted on. Lesley and Ate looked at Pratt, who looked at Steve Brody, who looked at Colonel Smith, who was trying not to look at the Romanian. The Romanian looked to Nate, Victoria and Tanya, who looked at each other and shifted in their seats. Normally they would have resented the implication that one of them could have committed a vicious double murder, but with the tuica overhead and the commanding tone of Fleet's presentation restricting their ability to offer any objection, they could only sit back and allow it to wash over them.

The band, meanwhile, was getting antsy. The Mop muttered something to the Girl, which sounded stupid and rabble-rousing. Kenny was leaning on the railing, his face propped up on his hand. The other twelve were wriggling about in the aisles, waiting.

Finally Fleet finished. He closed the volume, looked up and smiled. He knew.

He asked Steve Brody, "When you went to see Lyle Pendleton this morning, you heard a piece of music playing in his study?"

The young spy considered. He seemed to recall there was a piece playing, yes.

"A violin piece?"

"Sounded like it, yeah. I couldn't hear it very well, but I think there was a violin. Why?"

"What's he saying?" Hutton called down to us. He was having trouble making out the soft-spoken Steve from that far above.

"He said *he couldn't hear it very well*," shouted Fleet.

"Oh!" answered Hutton. "*Couldn't hear what very well?*"

Fleet thanked Steve for his assistance. "I suspect Lyle was listening to César Franck's *Violin Sonata in A* when you arrived. Or, as it is sometimes known on the street, *the Frank Sinatra*."

Hearing this, the crowd whispered amongst themselves, these whispers carrying all the way up to the balconies. Someone whispered, "Ol' Blue Eyes." Another whispered, "The King." A third whispered, "That's Elvis, you mook."

Fleet proceeded:

"Lyle figured out Chester's cryptic clue, and because of that he had to die. I thought, at first, you had done the deed, Mr. Pratt. You were there, were you not?"

Henry would have shrugged, but the dog leash kept him in check. "I didn't kill anyone."

"No, but you know who did. You saw the killer do it. You were searching the villa for the missing Romanian Rhapsody at the time."

"That's all I ever wanted, chief. The score. It's worth a bundle, that tune."

"And having failed to secure that tune, you're now intent on keeping silent in the hopes that the killer will reward you for your discretion. That is why you have fought us at every turn, misled us, impeded our investigation."

"Ask him if talking like a jazz roadie was part of that plan," I interjected. "Ask him why he talks that way. Why do you talk that way?" I demanded. Henry refused to sing.

Fleet left him to his reticence. "It's no matter. When you realize that the killer has no intention of paying you, perhaps then you will change your tune. I am correct, am I not, Tanya? You never intended to pay Henry Pratt?"

Tanya Saxon maintained her gaze. "And why should I pay Mr. Pratt anything?"

"As the silent partner in your crimes, of course. Tell me, what does a good murder accessory go for these days?"

Tanya flashed her pearly whites, the very asset that had earned her the honor of Miss Hoboken several centuries ago. "You probably hear this a lot, Mr. Fleet, but I have no idea what you are talking about."

"Of course you do." He included the rest of the room in the conversation. "I've been remiss in explaining one detail. As this handsome volume will attest, Franck's Sonata has another claim to fame, beyond its sobriquet. It was written for the wedding of Eugène Ysaÿe. As most of you know, Ysaÿe was one of the more talented violinists of his time and a composer in his own right. Franck gave him the sonata as a wedding gift, making Ysaÿe's anniversary a significant date in the piece's history. Eugène Ysaÿe was married on September 26, 1886. Or, as the Europeans would have it, 26 September 1886. 26/9/86.

"So what does this mean?" Fleet asked us. "Let's examine the mindset of Chester Callas leading up to his murder. He steps away during the banquet to a prearranged meeting place in the balcony. He doesn't know who he is meeting, only that they claim to have information on the third Romanian Rhapsody Nate Goody has falsely promised him. He goes, but his contact is not there. The phone rings. Or perhaps ringing is the wrong term. Does a silent ring still constitute a ring? That's a question for the philosophers, I suppose. The phone signals him. He picks up, and a voice speaks. Tanya Saxon's voice. He asks her where the score is. She says there is no score. Instead, she has brought him here to kill him. She has, in fact, already killed him, she says, poisoning his champagne during the banquet. He demands to know who she is, why she has done this. She tells him, but still he can't identify her among the guests. Then he sees the extension displayed. 26986. He has her number now. The poison, however, has begun to take effect. He looks at the digits again, and his mind races; his eidetic brain goes off on a tangent. 26/9/86, the date of Ysaÿe's anniversary, the wedding performance of Franck's Sonata. The Frank Sinatra, a piece Chester has played a thousand times himself.

"This doesn't help him. He takes out his penknife and jabs himself in the shoulder, to be sure the authorities don't mistake his death for an allergic reaction. And then, possibly by accident, or possibly not, he stumbles back and falls off the balcony.

"His last words, as he looks up from the table and sees John Hathaway bending over him, are the result of a strong intellect attempting to communicate the only information it has. His mind is too far fried to speak the extension. He mutters *Frank Sinatra* and dies. And so the mystery of those haunting words has begun."

I'd be willing to bet that the Pendleton Library had never been that silent.

Tanya Saxon spoke. She no longer balked.

(I always appreciate it when killers spill it—so much less tedious than waiting for the police to assemble their evidence and the attorneys to do their stuff.)

Tanya held nothing back. I suppose when you're six hundred and ninety years old you have nothing much to lose. "You're perfectly correct. I killed Chester Callas."

"Why?" I asked. I hadn't meant to speak, but sometimes you can't help it. "Did he do you wrong in a business deal?"

"No."

"Cheat you out of a violin? Make fun of the Miss Hoboken pageant? What?"

She stared out with her best cold, dead expression.

"Five years ago Chester Callas reviewed one of my husband's performances. My husband was somewhat younger than I," she mentioned. "He was second violin for the ensemble. Victoria will remember it; she played cello. Callas savaged the performance, spewing the majority of his venom on the second violin. On my husband. My husband gave up classical music after that, and sometime later, he gave up on me. I last heard that he was playing fiddle in a country-and-western band and had shacked up with a lady rodeo performer."

That was it? I thought. A bad review? I remember reading somewhere about a famous poet who had supposedly died from a bad review, but this was the first I had heard of an artist's wife murdering the reviewer five years later. I don't know what Chester said about the guy and his second-rate second-violin playing, but it couldn't have been any worse than what half my teachers said to me in school on a daily basis.

The old broad wasn't just formidable, she was nuts.

One final question remained. Enescu Fleet asked it: "I can almost understand your desire for vengeance against Chester Callas. But why Lyle? Even if he was threatening to unmask you, you had known him for three quarters of a century."

Tanya shrugged. She had no leash holding her back. "And I never really cared for him," she said.

These heartless words may have been the last we ever heard on a case well solved. As it happened, they weren't.

From up above, a husky voice commanded: "No one is to be moving!" which I took to be the Czech equivalent of "Nobody move!"

For Czechs were what we got—Czechs galore. Eight men had lined up one level above Hutton and two levels above the fighting Pendleton marching band.

Colonel Smith looked well pleased with the turnout. We should have realized that he would have more soldiers coming. Typically, the heads of small private armies have more than four men at their disposal. They have twelve men, at least.

His smug satisfaction didn't last long. He had barely time to smirk to himself before another shout rang through the library, this time from the fifth-story balcony.

This one said, "This is the police!" And by golly it was too. I spotted my old friend Sergeant Mustache and everything. "Drop your weapons!" he yelled down to us. I would have preferred he had phrased that differently.

Kenny, obeying the command, sprang to attention, bumping into his bottle of flaming liqueur. It rolled down the balcony's edge, bounced off a pillar and twirled to a halt. There, it tipped and wobbled on the ledge an instant, and then it was gone.

In a blur, I saw Ate standing right below it. I had just enough time to collide with her supple midsection before the drop. My tackle propelled us into the periodical section. The bottle hit and burst into flames not ten feet away.

"Sorry!" yelled Kenny, but it was too late for sorries.

A conflagration had broken out and was spreading fast, making the library much more of a barbecue pit than the founding architects had ever intended.

My initial reaction, after climbing back to my feet and helping Fleet's daughter to hers, was astonishment. Not astonishment over all the flames and smoke but over the inherent good in people. Instead of taking this opportunity to fill the authorities with hot lead, Smith's mercenaries had dashed to the scene of the fire. Some were helping to drag people to safety; others, together with their commanding officer, were attempting to smother the blaze with their jackets. Steve Brody and the Romanian assisted, three countries acting as one. The police were down from their balcony, and even the band had begun to lend a few drunken hands to assist.

Fire bells were ringing—what the library lacked in phone sound effects, it made up for in fire alarms—people were hacking and coughing, and Maltese were yapping. From a puff of smoke, Hutton bounded into our midst like a Vegas illusionist.

"I saw some extinguishers out in the hall," he said.

I followed him through the choking haze. I had trouble walking. In the dive for Ate, I had jammed my knee pretty bad. Returning with an extinguisher in each hand, we began to fight fire with—well, maybe not fire, but whatever you call that firefighting foam.

The first thing I saw once the flames began to abate was Tanya Saxon.

The old biddy was on the run across the fifth-story balcony above us. I would learn later that there was a secret set of steps down the back of the building, typically only authorized for use by library personnel. The police had used them to assemble their SWAT team, and it was these steps that Tanya hoped to ride to freedom.

The second thing I saw was a pair of rapid young figures coming up behind her. Lesley and Ate were hot on her trail.

They caught up to her at the middle balcony. There was a brief tussle, and then Tanya showed that she still had fight left in her old frame. She shook off Ate with a sharp dart to her right and avoided Lesley with a quick step and shuffle. The ladies weren't about to let her through that easily. Lesley snagged her pale, stockinged leg; Ate bounded onto her back; and the three went down in a heap behind the smoke and railings.

There was a wait of about ten seconds—it felt more like ten minutes—and then the scrum tottered back into view. My heart crashed into my throat. The girls were both on top of her—I don't know what was holding the old woman up—and that wasn't the worst of it. As the twirling ball of female flesh collided with the balcony railing, she managed to fling them off her back.

Ate flipped over the rail and just managed to snag the bar with both hands. Lesley was thrown farther afield. She somersaulted over the railing and landed fifteen feet to Ate's right, her tender little hand holding on by a single set of fingertips.

Before Hutton's and my staring eyes, the women in our lives were dangling two hundred feet off the ground.

I couldn't think. I couldn't move. Every staircase was engulfed in flame now. It didn't matter anyway. I could never reach them soon enough. Could I? I would have to try. I was already limping headlong into the smoke when I caught Hutton out of my peripheral vision.

He was running hard too but not toward the staircases. He was heading straight for the balcony under the girls. He bounded up on a desktop without breaking stride, sailed through the air and grabbed hold of the second-story railing. I never could have managed such a feat in a thousand tries, good knee or not.

He was up and over the railing in a split second and disappeared into the staircase above the flames.

He would never get there in time. And even if he did, he would only have time to save one of them.

I knew which one he would save, and I wanted to die.

Still unable to move, I watched as Ate struggled to improve her grip on the bar, and Lesley—

Lesley lost hers.

She had fallen perhaps two inches when a hand shot down out of the darkness and grabbed hold: Hutton's hand. He pulled her up to safety.

They slumped over on the floor on the good side of the balcony, and a few seconds later Ate joined them, flipping herself back over the railing and landing in a splat a few feet away.

I could see her lips move and wondered what she said to him. Hutton later told me it was: "Thanks…I'm okay too!"

26 — Romanian Rhap-up

The following evening, I was standing backstage in the Rondo Auditorium. I was holding Pixie, who, despite two baths, still smelled like a smoked Malta sausage. As I stood there trying not to sniff her, I glanced out at the happy crowd and as I glanced, felt happy myself.

My beautiful fiancée was sitting in the first row. Even though the fire had left most of the Pendleton Library unsinged, we had mutually decided that holding our wedding reception there would feel rather anticlimactic now. We had plenty of time to choose a less exciting venue—the Congo maybe—we weren't picky.

Next to Lesley sat Hutton and Ate. They were holding hands and had become closer, emotionally, in the last few hours than I had ever seen them. At first this puzzled me, since it was Lesley and not Ate Hutton had rescued. But then my sharp insight into human psychology showed me the way.

Her whole life, Ate had lived in the shadow of that superhuman Enescu Fleet. He was always there for her, always saving her. That was great, but for once she wanted to show that she could save someone too, and she had done that thanks to Hutton's neglect.

She had saved herself.

Ironically, scoring points hadn't been Hutton's intention at all. After his heroic effort yesterday, I asked him why he had gone for my fiancée and not the woman he cared for, and he explained that he had to pick one and Lesley needed him more than Ate. It was basic numbers. Ate had two hands on the bar, Lesley only one. His calculation had proved correct, and I thanked God that it had.

He also cleared up one last mystery for me. Continuing our session from the previous night, he asked if I still wanted to know what it was that Chester had done to him in their youth: the thing that had made Hutton hate him more than the average right-thinking citizen might.

I said of course I still wanted to know, and he replied, simply, that Chester was the one who had told him he was adopted. He had found out somehow, and waiting for the perfect moment one day in the nursery, he had let Hutton have it. That was why Hutton despised him. It was the control aspect more than anything. Like any bully, Chester had imposed a power over him by imparting his secret. Now that the case was done, Hutton felt comfortable getting this off his chest.

That's what he said, anyway, but I knew the real reason he opened up: little Chester had chipped a portion off Hutton's trust in family that day, that feeling of safety we all need and desire. Today, Hutton had gotten it back, plus some.

You could see it in the grip of two hands.

Some movement on stage suggested that the concert was about to begin. Steve Brody, still performing under the name of Sergei Brodovitch, would be jamming with Rachel Barton Pine and Victoria Walters.

Victoria, I learned, had confessed everything to Nate Goody about her trickery with his violin, and Nate had forgiven her. This magnanimous attitude he also extended to the band. Kenny and crew had been expelled but with no charges pending from the college. The dean wanted to forget all about it, which was his specialty.

Henry Pratt would likely be getting off with a suspended sentence himself; for it was Henry, in the end, who had nabbed Tanya Saxon. During the fire and still bound with Pixie's leash, he had cut Tanya off as she fled the building and taken her out with a head-butt to the stomach. He didn't even have to risk using those wonderful, drum-playing hands of his.

I glanced up to see Enescu Fleet at my side. He was back in his tuxedo, looking as sharp as ever. "Sorry I'm late," he said, "had to see a Romanian about a score."

"Score—"

"The third Romanian Rhapsody by George Enescu."

I gaped. "You mean—"

"It was real. Lyle gave it to me when we first arrived, and I just gave it to the Romanian. He would have stayed on and thanked you, but he had to get going. Already Colonel Smith's constant job offers were beginning to make him uncomfortable. Smith's left too, by the way."

I wasn't concerned with the colonel's travel plans. "I thought the score was a hoax?"

"Lyle allowed Nate to believe it was while he figured out if the score was the thing causing all the intrigue at the Institute. I suppose in a way it was, and in a way it wasn't."

"So the world has a third Romanian Rhapsody now?"

"Technically speaking, a single Romanian has it. Soon Romania will have it and sometime after that, the world."

"And you had it all along—"

"Actually, no. Your uncle had it all along, the other George."

"My unc—?"

"I gave it to him for safekeeping last night. I had to keep it out of the wrong hands, and who better to trust with such a charge than a congressman? By the way, he asked me to thank you for helping him get away. It was a little awkward, because he had come to the banquet with every intention of beating Chester Callas within an inch of his life."

I tried to absorb these words, but nothing doing. "He had every intention of what now?"

"Beating Chester Callas within an inch of his life. By the time he arrived, though, Chester had already gone quite a few inches past his life, and beating him then would not have been seemly, especially for a congressman."

I was gaping again. "Why did Uncle George want to beat up Chester Callas?"

"Evidently, as a youth, Chester had interned with your uncle on one of his first political campaigns: a job he got on the strength of having been at school with you. Not only did Chet share secrets with your uncle's opponent, your uncle strongly suspected him of pilfering the petty cash accounts. He disappeared soon after that, only to reemerge back in England some years later as a consultant to a record label, a position he'd earned on the strength of having been an intern to a US congressman. Your uncle eventually heard about this and got him fired, but he had always harbored a quiet yearning for physical violence against the man: a promise he made sure to relay to Chester's ex-employer. Whether he would have actually gone through with it, given his position, I doubt, but it amused him to entertain the possibility."

So that was why Chester had turned pale and run at the mention of my Uncle George? I thought I was the only one who did that.

"That was why he offered to help sneak the score," said Fleet. "I think he felt guilty for his primal urges. I don't know why you dislike him, Johnny. He seemed a nice fellow to me. And he looks just like Frank Sinatra."

I declined to go into my uncle's apparent niceness. That could be another question for the philosophers. On the Sinatra side, I definitely dug Fleet's opinion. I commented once again on the number of Frank Sinatra details in this case, and he agreed there had been a few, hadn't there? He supposed that when you go looking for a figure larger than life, you're bound to see the man's legacy popping up everywhere.

I could dig that too. I had my own experience with larger-than-life figures. The one in my life had just removed a clarinet from a slender case. I stared at this as he adjusted knobs and switches and other contraptions. "Are you really going to do this?" I asked.

"Perform with Rachel Barton Pine, Sergei Whosit and Victoria Walters? Need you ask?"

I supposed I needn't. Nonetheless, we had been through this before, and I had to know: "You can actually play the clarinet, right? This isn't more bravado, like you pretending to be a descendant of George Enescu?"

He paused. "Only one way to find out," he replied.

And on that note, he stepped out into the spotlight, where men like him belong.

Further Reading

If you enjoyed *Fleeting Note*, you'll be delighted to learn that there are two previous books in the series: *Fleeting Memory* and *Fleeting Glance.* John Hathaway and Lesley Darlington also appear in the earlier adventure, *Five Star Detour.*

www.ingramcontent.com/pod-product-compliance
Lightning Source LLC
Chambersburg PA
CBHW020611310726
48979CB00008B/1428/J
* 9 7 8 0 9 9 1 2 3 2 4 5 1 *